TWISTED ROOTS

Also by J.J. Fryer

Beneath the Surface series
Inner Reflection
Fragile Treasure

BENEATH THE SURFACE BOOK THREE
TWISTED ROOTS

J. J. FRYER

Twisted Roots
Beneath the Surface Book Three

Copyright © 2025
J. J. Fryer

All rights reserved. No part of this publication may be reproduced, stored in a retrieval system or transmitted in any form or by any means, electronic, mechanical, photocopying, recording or otherwise, without the prior written permission of the publisher.

The information, views, opinions and visuals expressed in this publication are solely those of the author(s) and do not reflect those of the publisher. The publisher disclaims any liabilities or responsibilities whatsoever for any damages, libel or liabilities arising directly or indirectly from the contents of this publication.

Published by Ouroborus Book Services
www.ouroborusbooks.com

Cover Design by Sabrina RG Raven
www.sabrinargraven.com

To Mum, happy birthday. I wish you were here to see this.

1: ECHOES ALL AROUND

All the sounds around me were muffled out by the thunderous beat of my heart. People shouted back at me to watch me where I was going and sweat gleamed on everyone's arms from the evening humidity. Half of it drenched the sleeves of my denim jacket. Bile crept up my throat. The crowd of people continued to build around the narrow corner where the electronics store sat. My feet propelled me forward as the news report from just a few minutes ago whispered darkly back. A feeling similar to claustrophobia followed immediately after.

'Police are looking for a girl about thirteen with a platinum-blond lightning streak in her hair.'

But it wasn't me, I reminded myself. It was Cassie, my identical sister. Why would she set me up like this?

Is she the one who ended Aiden's life? If so, why?

'Hey, that's Ana! The girl the cops are after. Get her!' Maggie pointed. Her brunette hair gleamed in the bright, angelic light from the nearby stores. An angry growl uncurled itself up my throat to behind my teeth. The swarm of people that surrounded Maggie stared at me with hate-filled eyes. Seconds later, they bulldozed around Maggie and chased after me. A couple of drivers blared their horns at the people who were on the road.

Another set of feet raced up the road too.

I quickly ducked to the side of a black lamppost and my feet teetered on the edge of the gutter. Eerily bright light reigned over the broken pieces of concrete. The furious mob took their phones out. I cupped my hands over my eyes so that no one could take a picture of me while they pushed and shoved each other for the perfect shot. Someone dragged me into a nearby alley. The crowd of people were still there, talking amongst themselves. Fear cried out to get away, but the stranger held me back, anchoring my arm in place.

'Let go of me.' I tried to wriggle out of their grip. A flash of Fletcher's red hair ran across my line of sight.

'Hey, take it easy,' Fletcher said. He kept his voice to a whisper, to avoid attracting any more attention this way.

'How am I supposed to take it easy when you surprise a person like that?' My eyes travelled down to my arm. Fletcher's hand was still clamped around it like a vice. He released his grip. 'And not sure if you heard but everyone is looking for me.'

'So, we'll hide out at the Arcade. I always go there when I want to avoid my family.'

'Do they always find you?'

Fletcher's eyes turned away from me, a little crestfallen. 'Yeah.'

A building in the shape of a giant tooth caught my attention from across the road.

'How about there?'

Fletcher turned around to see what I was looking at. 'The dentist office, are you crazy? That would be the last place anyone would look for a kid... oh.' He caught on to what I was thinking.

'Let's go.' I raised my hands to cover the sides of my face again.

'Wait, we're going to need disguises,' Fletcher suggested. 'Stay here, in case they come snooping around here.'

He walked over to a convenience store across the road. Black metal stands with postcards in them spun around in the gentle breeze. He came back a couple of minutes later with a pair of dark-tinted sunglasses and bucket hats that said:

WELCOME TO OPAL CREEK
A PLACE WHERE TREASURED MEMORIES ARE DISCOVERED

My eyes looked at the bold white letters and a picture of a family having a picnic by the Jade River, which got its name because the water was always jade in colour. It was a little on the nose, but at least people would remember the name. The only memories that this place had given me were ones where I discovered my powers, secrets that I couldn't tell my parents, and I couldn't go home anymore. Nobody would talk to my parents because people trusted news anchors. Would Mum and Dad know that their daughter could never do anything that evil? How could they help me with the fact that my body occupied another soul?

The endless questions that bounced around in my head made it hard to focus, even if I covered my ears. The couple that sat on the red gingham picnic blanket looked so happy as their kid ran across the bright green grass. The kid's plaits flew behind her in an invisible breeze.

I hope to be as happy as they are soon.

'Thanks,' I said sarcastically as I grabbed the hat and sunglasses from Fletcher. 'Why are you running away with me? I'm the one the police want.'

'Because that's what friends do, now hurry up and put on your disguise.'

A lightness filled up my lungs at Fletcher not leaving me to face this drama alone. One look at the disguise made me feel like a cat about to take a bath — I wasn't happy about it. These items didn't make a disguise, not to mention that the hat was tacky. I groaned through the humiliation as I shoved the hat over my head and quickly slid on the glasses.

Fletcher put on his disguise — one of those weird pairs of sunglasses with a moustache that dangled at the bottom. 'Does this make me manly?'

'No,' I answered bluntly. It was at times like these that maybe a girl would've been a better companion.

'Thanks for your honesty.'

'You're welcome.'

Fletcher peeked around the corner to make sure the coast was clear. We power-walked from the alley across a pedestrian crossing. More people flooded around the eager group that wanted a photo of me. Fruit stands were blocked by them. The front of the dentist's office had charming French shutters that were painted white, just like the building. Streetlights projected light from across the front of the dentist's office. The streetlights bore a striking resemblance to those described in my favourite book as a child, about a girl who walked into a wardrobe and discovered a magical land on the other side. The name of the dentist's office, *Pearly White Smile Dentistry*, could be seen on the short metallic sign guarding the front yard that was out of reach of the light's grasp. Fuchsia roses relaxed in their two-by-one-foot flower beds on either side of the few steps that led to the small veranda. We crept up the steps to the front door, but it was locked.

'Come on, there's got to be a back door, right?' Fletcher asked. He pressed his face to the glass door.

'Why do I get the sense that you're enjoying this *way* more than I am?'

He replied with a sly grin.

We turned around from the door and heard something smash to the ground inside the building. My blood ran cold. My eyes caught Fletcher's face go as pale as the building itself.

I raised a concerned brow at him.

Fletcher saw my expression and his face returned colour to his cheeks. 'I'm good. I was just... surprised was all.'

'You know it's okay if you're scared.'

'SCARED!' He quickly lowered his voice; he seemed to forget for a second that everyone around me could turn me in, so that there would be one less scary person out in the world. He gritted his teeth as he took a quick glance to see if anyone had paid attention. When the coast was clear, he continued his rant. 'I was not *scared*, I was just faking it so you would be comfortable.'

'I would be comfortable if you just react however you wanted to. You don't have to hide your feelings. You know that being a man means you don't have to hide your feelings and protect me — that state of mind is so dated.'

'I didn't say that I was like this because of that?'

I started to walk down the wheelchair access ramp. There might have been a back door that someone snuck through. Fletcher remained where he was.

'You didn't have to,' I called back to him.

He raced after me. 'Why are you acting like this?'

'Because you have no idea how it feels when someone tells you that since I'm on the autism spectrum, I can't understand or have no emotions.' The weight that was in my chest pulled me down. It kept me rooted to one place. I couldn't move. Maybe the weight of the memory didn't want me to? My magic wanted me to let out the energy that bubbled inside. I had some control over my powers, but not all the time.

Just above our heads, pale wisps of cloud, that moments ago drifted of their own free will, swarmed over and darkened into a lead grey. Seconds later, ice cold rain started to drown us.

'I don't understand them like everyone else, Fletcher. Emotions aren't black and white—they're grey. Whenever I hear people assume that I don't have or understand emotions, it hurts. And now, I have these freaky powers to show what I'm feeling every time I think about it.'

The silence deafened after that.

I had to reach through a circular hole in the tall wooden gate that separated the front and back of the dental office. The latch on the other side of the gate was cold. The rain had stopped, but the emotions still lingered. I pushed open the gate, and Fletcher and I crept through before I passed it to Fletcher to close. The gate slammed shut, which made me jump.

I stared back at him. 'Why couldn't you just close it quietly?'

He clenched his teeth, then shrugged his shoulders. 'Sorry.'

I turned back around and scoffed, annoyed with him.

Shards of gravel crunched under our feet.

The back of the dentist's office had a little light, just like the front, except there were no lanterns nearby. There was, however, a ghostly white light of the full moon hovering over a small carpark. Beside it were a few mango trees. Rotten mangoes littered the road, probably from the fruit bats that couldn't resist a snack. The stench from the fruit clogged our sense of smell. A dumpster stood around the corner from me. I was about to turn my head in the direction of the moon.

Fletcher covered his mouth and ran in front of me. 'Hey, Ana, you should come and see this.'

'What is it?' I asked, annoyed.

But my short burst of anger settled. He glided his hand over a part of the railing that was crushed by someone—or something—with a very strong grip.

'What could have done this?'

My eyes flicked to Fletcher's for just a moment. They trailed across the railing where a pencil-thin scratch scored the rail. There were no other marks on the railing, but tiny marks continued up and across the wall, just like Cassie's locker and the ground in Ancient Egypt.

The back door to the dental office had been forced open. What was in there? An eerie feeling washed over me. *I don't want to go in there.* Fletcher peeked behind the door to see the damage that was done, and his face quivered slightly with the same emotion I felt. He physically pushed me inside. It was something he usually did to make me take more risks, or in this case, because he was scared to go in first. The pale light from outside highlighted the brightly coloured flooring inside. It could have been white or sky-blue; it was hard to tell at nighttime.

A high-pitched creak called out behind me. I turned and saw Fletcher close the door behind him.

'They should really get the hinges oiled,' he suggested.

I rolled my eyes. 'Could you make any more noise?' The words were as restrained as I could handle at that moment, which was very little.

We walked down the hall. I reached out to touch the walls, which were cold, and little lumps of paint glided under my hands.

Darkness surrounded us everywhere.

My hands ran over a round, metallic doorknob. This must have been where the dentist checked out their patients' teeth. The scent of the alcohol-based sanitiser was strong even with the door closed. *I haven't been to the dentist since last year.* The memory of him scraping my teeth with the mirror and hook still gave me nightmares.

I felt another doorknob a few paces after the last one.

Something smashed on the floor.

I quickly removed my hand from what felt like the doorframe, and crashed into Fletcher behind me. He grunted in pain.

'Who's there?' a young, terrified voice asked.

'We're just playing hide and seek with some people,' Fletcher answered.

'Go hide somewhere else. You can't hide here tonight, especially not tonight,' the voice replied.

'Why not tonight?' I asked.

'Because it's a full moon.' The person didn't speak for a moment before they said, 'I shouldn't have told you that. Leave NOW!'

'We're not going to hurt you.'

'But I might hurt you and your friend.'

'Oh, trust me. She can take care of herself,' said Fletcher.

I started to walk toward the scared voice. Hopefully, if I showed myself to the person, they wouldn't be afraid of me.

Fletcher put a hand on my shoulder. 'What are you doing?'

'Trust me, this might work.'

'Might work?' Fletcher whispered. 'Why are you now deciding to take risks in dangerous moments?'

I ignored Fletcher as I started to quietly creep toward the scared person. Something scuffed against my right foot. With darkness around us, I squatted down and used my hand to feel my way down the wall to assist me. Once I was on the floor, I circled my arms around the general area where I heard the noise. Now I knew how a lighthouse felt when its light searched for lost ships out at sea. Frustration started to build up inside me. Where was it? It had to be around here somewhere. One of my fingers grazed a small object that was cold to the touch. I scraped it off the floor. At the same time, I heard something slip away from the first item that I found.

I reached under my leg and found something that felt like a chain. *Claw marks on the door. Superhuman strength. Afraid of the full moon.* I needed light to confirm my theory. The other item that I held had different lengths to it. It was hard to know what the image was in the dark. I waved my hands in front of me to know if I would bump into anything or not. And surely enough, my foot struck a large pot with a plant.

Next thing I knew, Fletcher bumped into me, and I almost landed in the pot plant.

'Hey, watch it!' I exclaimed.

'I'm trying. It's hard seeing in the dark, you know,' he rebutted. Fletcher took a sharp intake of breath as the other person in the room cried out in pain.

'Watch where you place your feet, you big oaf,' the scared voice snapped, 'and didn't I tell you to get lost?'

'You did, but maybe there's a way we can all share this building,' I suggested.

I placed both the items in one hand and searched for a source of light with the other. There were stacks of paper placed on a flat surface that reached just below the level of my waist. My fingers danced over a computer's keyboard. They also brushed across a book that had a smooth, felt-like texture. My hand touched a mug filled with pens located next to the computer. A desk lamp with a long neck was the next thing that my arm knocked into. I needed to find the switch.

Someone crashed into a set of wooden blinds. They didn't sound as melodic as wind chimes.

'Here's some light,' Fletcher said, as he bashed the sheet of blinds against the window.

'What are you doing, do you want to get us caught?'

I finally found a small, concave rectangular button and pushed it to one side. Part of the room coloured in a warm, yellow light. I uncurled my hand with the items in it, both of which were gold. The chain was now in a small mountain in my palm. Each of the links were about the size of one of my phalanges.

'No, don't touch that!' the unknown voice yelped in pain. 'I need to find my amulet. It's the only thing that can save us both.'

'What do you mean?' I asked.

'Oww, what sharp nails you have,' Fletcher cried out. He rubbed one hand over the other. The two of us walked away from the desk back toward where we started from. A potted fern stood where the hallway ended and the desk began. Grey fabric chairs peeked around a corner a few paces ahead of me.

I turned my attention back to the other item. It was a pendant in the shape of a creature's head. It appeared almost jackal-like. The only time I'd seen a creature like this was when we were in Ancient Egypt. When the silver-masked girl, who turned out to be Imogen, cursed a group of men that worked on the pyramids—one of them being a kind man who took Fletcher and me in at the time—into such creatures.

My mind flashed back to when I created a portal without the assistance of a Key lime pie to get us out of there. Could I have done things differently then? I had to get out of there, even if it meant we failed the mission to stop those kids from ruining the timeline. It was a painful moment to relive. The memory faded away like waves after a storm.

'Hey, Ana, what's that on the back?' Fletcher asked, as he gently woke me out of my dream-like state. He must've turned the pendant over while I was distracted.

I shook my head and saw what he was pointing to. A single hieroglyph of an eye.

'It's the Eye of Horus. The Ancient Egyptians used this as a symbol of protection.'

'Where did you learn to read hieroglyphs?' Fletcher asked.

'From the amazing thing known as the Internet.' The engraving didn't look new, like it was passed down from generations.

Hurt continued to pour out of the other person's mouth; it made me lose my train of thought. A light howl immediately followed the cry of pain.

Panic invaded my mind. 'It's a wolf.'

Fletcher caught onto what I realised. 'It could be?'

'It's both a wolf and whoever we've tried to talk to,' I whispered. My shoulders slumped forward with regret.

'*Ana! RUN!*' Fletcher screamed at me, but it was muffled by my emotions. The wind churned outside. The other person's breath suddenly changed into a rumble. Their hands had chunks of short, tan-coloured fur on them. Fletcher crashed into me. His eyes flared with terror. He tried to wake me from my apologetic state.

'*It was all my fault,*' a voice in my head echoed.

'I should've fixed everything before we left.' My voice croaked as tears swam to the front of my eyes. I saw a blurred image of the unnamed person's dark hair as it changed to match the rest of their fur. Fletcher was about to say something. The snout of the were-creature emerged from under the desk and its claws scratched into the wood. Fletcher pulled me into the room's first door on the right, which was ajar, and stood guard.

Fine threads of moonlight streamed through the frosted glass window at the back of the room.

I wiped the tears that poured down my face with the sleeve of my denim jacket.

On the bench next to the dentist chair lay a jar. Half of the lollipops were gone. Either someone forgot to refill the container or someone was very hungry.

Images of Asim floated in front of me. His kind eyes and gentleness warmed my soul.

'These amulets must protect were-creatures from the effects of the full moon. Without it, they will transform into that.' I gestured to the space outside the door. 'A priest or priestess must've forged and blessed them after we left.'

'So how do we get out of here in one piece? Wait until the sun comes up?' Fletcher turned away from the doorway to look at me for an answer.

Silence filled the room.

My eyes wandered past Fletcher. The were-creature ran for the doorway. Its ears were long and sharply pointed. This creature wasn't a wolf, but a jackal exactly like Anubis, the Egyptian God of the Afterlife. Fletcher caught the fearful look in my eyes and turned around to see what I saw. The creature leaped across the small corridor and was about to enter the room.

Luckily, Fletcher slammed the door, but it wasn't entirely shut and the jackal-like beast was strong.

Fletcher slid back from the force of the wild creature. 'I could use some help here.'

I needed to take some deep breaths.

I couldn't.

My best friend needs me now.

I scraped myself up off the floor. With our combined strength, we pushed the animal back as best we could. Then it was gone.

'Well, that was easy,' Fletcher said, until one of the creature's long limbs broke through the gap. It pushed in between the space and pounced into the room. The animal's silvery-white eyes found us and we were trapped in its line of sight. It then leapt on top of us and my heart galloped inside my chest.

Fletcher and I were sandwiched between the creature's front legs and the floor. Its warm, lollipop-scented breath drifted between us. None of us knew what to do next. A golden light burst from Fletcher's wrist. The were-creature jumped back and we were free from its deadly grasp.

We tried to stare at the light, but it was too bright to see what caused it.

'Thank you, ma'am, we'll take it from here,' a voice replied to someone outside the dentistry.

I opened my eyes again to see whose voice that belonged to. The answer came in flashes of red and blue light that danced against the window.

'Fletcher, we have to go! The police are here!' I caught sight of the sun bracelet that Clara had given him. It produced the same heavenly glow that was aimed at the creature. Soon, the menacing being before us shrank down to my height.

'What's that?' a deep gruff voice asked.

'I don't know. Let's find out,' the first new voice replied, softer than the other.

Someone or something pushed the door open even further. In the place of the huge monster crouched a person with a plain white crop top, dark denim jacket and matching jeans that were shredded at the knees. The radiant light went out completely.

'What's going on?' the person in the crop top asked. They shook in confusion. Their voice also matched the one Fletcher and I spoke to earlier. I threaded the golden jackal pendant through the gold chain and clasped it behind their neck.

'Don't you remember turning into a were-creature and almost having us for dinner?' Fletcher asked.

The confused person rubbed the back of their head. 'The last thing I remember is some punk kid ripped my amulet off, and I took shelter here so no one could get hurt. I can't believe it happened again.'

'What's your name?' I asked.

'It's Sami, and you are?' the other person—Sami—replied. Their hand squeezed around the amulet.

'Hey, it's the girl from the news,' one of the officers announced as he came through the door with his torch pointed at our eyes.

Fletcher and I turned to each other with a shared expression of panic before running for the door where the officer stood.

The other officer appeared. She wore a dark-coloured hijab. 'Please stop, we just want to talk with you.'

I just managed to squeeze by both officers after Fletcher. Then the male officer grabbed the collar of my denim jacket. 'Let me go!' I yelled.

Fletcher's shoes screeched to a halt on the plastic flooring and he ran back toward the officer with the vice-like grip. He smashed a foot on the man's polished shoes. The officer yelled out in pain, but it was enough to release me to tend to his injured foot.

'Thanks, you're a lifesaver,' I sighed in relief.

'Don't thank me yet. We still have to find a place to hide. Fortunately, I know just the place.'

We rushed out of the dentist's office, and I followed Fletcher blindly into the night.

2: SCOOP OF THE DAY

We ran at least three blocks down from the dentistry. A convenience store sign almost distracted me with its white, orange and dark green sign. No one in the apartment building behind the store were roused by the ultra-bright sign, or the police siren. Aromatic scents of curry and cinnamon sugar came from the Indian restaurant and churro shop across the road.

My stomach protested with hunger. A bus pulled up to a stop half a kilometre ahead of us.

Fletcher came to an abrupt stop a few paces ahead of it, and I crashed into his back. The few people that got off the bus swerved around us. They were either too into the music they listened to or were caught up in their own heads. I could relate to the latter.

'Here,' he proclaimed.

'What do you mean here? Next time, can you tell me when you're going to stop, so I can be better prepared?' I grumbled. Tension pinched up my neck. My fingers massaged the spot.

He ignored my suggestion. 'I used to come here when my parents fought, when they were still together.'

I placed my hand on his shoulder. Above us was a black hole sign, with indigo and purple neon lights. White neon illuminated the name of the building.

OBSIDIAN VORTEX ARCADE

A siren wailed behind us. I took a little peek behind me and saw the police car from earlier. Fletcher quickly grabbed my wrist and dragged me into the alley in between the arcade and the ice-cream shop. Once the car cruised on by, he told me to hide behind the dumpster.

'Why?' I asked, not budging from my spot until I got an answer.

'I know the owner. She's like a sister I never had. I'll ask her for help. I won't say that I'm hiding the girl that destroyed a young boy's life.'

'Good call.' Nerves rattled in my bones. It was too risky for anyone else to get involved with my situation.

'What did you expect?'

I rolled my eyes and ducked behind the dumpster with a giant rectangular red lid. Two pairs of lights shone above the back door to the ice-cream shop, and another was above the arcade's side entrance. They blinked once, twice, then three times. This pattern repeated three times. Fletcher knocked on the door. The sound he made sounded like rain.

Pitter-patter.

Pitter-patter.

Pitter-patter.

'Hey, Roxy, open up!'

The door shoved open, but it was stuck. The person on the other side of it rammed the door a second time and it crashed into the wall. A woman wearing long, dark braids and a headband with a galaxy print on it stood in the doorway.

'What's up, pocket rocket?' the woman asked.

Pocket rocket? I'll have to ask Fletcher how he got that name.

'Can you turn off these lights?' Fletcher pointed to the lights above the door. 'My friend is autistic and isn't good with flashing lights.'

'Is this that boy you brought here last time?' Roxy asked, her jade-coloured eyes filled with hope.

At the mention of 'the boy', Fletcher's cheeked flushed bright red.

'No, this is just a friend of mine,' he managed to say as the colour of his cheeks returned to normal.

'I believe you.' Roxy was disappointed and disappeared from the doorway, and a few seconds later the lights above the door were switched off.

'PSST!' Fletcher called out.

I emerged from my hiding spot next to the dumpster. A broken bottle lay next to it, and was hit with a show of bright, neon lights. The arcade was lit up in a rainbow-coloured glow that immediately made my head pulse. Loud music spilled from the arcade's open door, which made my teeth grate against each other. I threw my hands over my ears to block out the noise. All around the arcade were different signs that related to outer space.

On the left was a café with a large neon sign of the sun on the wall. Parents partly relaxed with cups of coffee in hand as they watched their kids wear themselves out on the games. Others watched a group of kids climb an obstacle course three storeys high, with smiles on their faces. One kid slurped a slushie too quickly, then he put down his drink and cried out, 'BRAINFREEZE!'

Something ached in the pit of my stomach; the pain made me twitch uncomfortably. It was like happiness was taken from me, and it had been. I couldn't go back to my regular life until I cleared my name. An image of Cassie floated to the front of my brain. *I have to find her and ask why she framed me for something I didn't do.*

As I drifted away with my thoughts, I lost sight of Fletcher and his friend. I looked to the opposite side of the arcade and noticed a court surrounded by a large white net. Inside were people throwing balls with pictures of asteroids on them.

On one side of the court was a basketball game with a picture of Saturn on a sign. At the other end was a ticket machine that spewed out tickets.

'Hey A, over here,' Fletcher called out. It sounded like he was behind me. I turned around and saw him and Roxy a few feet away on a dance machine with the sign for Venus in between them. Roxy touched her phone to a machine, and it glowed green after she moved her phone away.

'Ready for your defeat this time, Fletch?' Roxy asked. A smirk appeared on her face.

'Do I get this place if you lose for the third time?' Fletcher responded.

'I don't go down that easily,' she answered back.

Fletcher tilted his head from side to side and stretched his arms and legs. Roxy's eyes were laser-focused. The game started and they both began in sync, crossing their legs left and right.

Something caught my eye. A few games over from the Saturn basketball game was an arcade machine with a pair of clear Perspex-like goggles attached to it. Above the machine was a sign with a picture of Pluto. I shuffled around the side where there was the name of the game printed on it.

ARCTIC PIRANHAS TWO

Déjà vu festered inside me as I remembered being in the exact game. I was about to be eaten by a piranha that lived in the Arctic. I shrugged the feeling from my shoulders. The night wore on and, according to the clocks shaped like rocket ships on every wall of the establishment, everyone left by ten-thirty.

Fletcher found me and told me that he and Roxy had been neck and neck right to the end, until she couldn't do a dance move. It was called the Twister, a move where you had to spin a few times. Then, in the final pose, you had to contort your body so that your legs were opposite to where you stood at the start of the game, then you needed to place your arms on the front and back spaces and stay squatted in that position for seven seconds.

He said that Roxy had terrible balance. Fletcher's eyes lit up when he mentioned that one day he'd own the arcade.

Roxy laughed and called back from behind him, 'Not until you graduate university with a business degree.'

We followed Roxy to a door marked *Quiet Room*. It had five glow-in-the-dark star stickers arranged in the shape of a star.

She placed her hand on the small round doorknob and turned to face me. I turned my head down avoid her gaze. 'This is where a few kids, mostly Fletcher, come to crash if they need a place to stay if they are having a hard time at home. It's empty at the moment, and if you need anything, I live in the unit out the back.' Delicate reassurance warmed me on the inside. 'Fletcher will show you around. Goodnight, you two.'

'Night,' Fletcher said louder than I did.

On the right of the room was a large white locker. I twisted the dial that served as the doorknob. It popped open and I looked inside and saw a very organised arrangement of things people would need when a person stayed overnight somewhere: sleeping bags, pillows, toiletries, personal hygiene items, towels and even pairs of pyjamas in multiple sizes.

'Mind if I use the shower first? My bracelet thing that Clara gave me is hurting my wrist.' Fletcher tapped his index finger on his wrist and immediately regretted it. Clara—Mother Nature's close friend and witch—had been the only other person, aside from

Fletcher, who believed that I wouldn't have harmed Aiden. She gave us these magical bracelets from her very own spell book and said they would protect us from any danger that Mother Nature sent our way. Clara didn't realise that they could protect us from much more than what Mother Nature sent after me.

I went over and flicked the switch. The room burst to life with light. Fletcher scratched at his wrist, which was red and burnt. 'Has this happened before?'

'No. It only started to happen after I used it against that were-creature kid.'

Concern clouded my face. 'Maybe your bracelet contains some kind of solar energy?'

'Cool!' Fletcher exclaimed.

'And that's the aftermath.' I pointed to his wrist.

'Oh, so what do I do to make this go away?'

'Try some aloe vera?'

Fletcher grabbed a towel and left the room.

I stared down at the bracelet I was given. Unlike Fletcher's, which had the positions of the sun, mine had the phases of the moon on it. I spun it around, and wondered what it could do. A loud crash from outside snapped me out of my thoughts. I went over to the window and peeked through the curtain.

Someone who worked at the ice-cream shop across the alley threw giant bags of rubbish into the dumpster, then slammed the lid shut once they were done. The employee turned her face. Cassie. It took a great deal of restraint for me to stay still. I imagined that I sent a tornado at her that would've thrown her in the dumpster. How was she able to carry on with life after what she did to Aiden? When did she even get a job?

She was about to look in my direction. Fletcher startled me and told me the bathroom was free. I looked back at the alley. Cassie had disappeared.

The next day, we restocked the prize area, cleaned the tables and refilled the ticket machines. I was so preoccupied by that I hadn't had time to construct a plan to confront Cassie. *How does Fletcher do it?* I stared at the clock on the wall. It told me that it was two o'clock in the afternoon. The arcade had just hosted a kids' birthday party.

Roxy asked Fletcher to take out the rubbish. He scrunched up his face in disgust. Who wanted to handle a rubbish bag full of sausage rolls that kids had thrown up? An idea sparked in my head.

'I'll give him a hand,' I told Roxy.

'Why? I don't need any help.'

'Just trust me.'

Roxy allowed it. If we stayed here, the least we could do was help out. With my new hat and sunglasses that Fletcher gave me, no one would recognise me. A rush of determination pumped through my body.

I pushed the door open for Fletcher. He replied by looking at me strangely. I didn't let it bother me.

The sky was light blue. Pale gold light washed across it. It was like an art piece on display at a gallery.

Fletcher's words interrupted me. 'Thanks for the help. You okay?'

'Hmm, yeah, I just love to stare at the sky. It makes

me forget about everything for a while.'

I heard footsteps coming from the opposite direction. The footsteps belonged to Cassie. My hand squeezed Fletcher's wrist as I dragged him behind the dumpster. His face blistered red with rage. We watched as she approached the door and then pulled it open. As soon as she passed the threshold, I grabbed Fletcher's wrist again and ran to catch up to her before the door closed. We made it with seconds to spare. I wedged my foot in between the door and frame and threw it open for us to get inside.

The first thing I noticed when the door closed behind us were the pale blue tiles. The second was an old woman with a dome of white hair. She blocked my view as Cassie walked away.

'This is how you show up for your first day? By being late?'

'You must think we're someone—' I started, then Fletcher jumped in to finish my sentence.

'What I think she meant to say was... you must think we forgot to set an alarm on our phones to remind us to get here on time.'

The woman just stared at us for a minute. 'Don't let that happen again, or you'll both be fired!'

'You got it.' Fletcher chuckled.

'Shirts are in the here.' The woman didn't look as she rotated a door handle to her right.

After she left the hallway, we went into the room and changed.

Fletcher and I came out of the dressing room with the same light blue polo shirts on, *The Chillin' Penguin* logo stitched in white on the left side of the shirt. It was a penguin relaxing in a deck chair with sunglasses on, an icy drink in hand and an umbrella perched just behind it. Above that, the name of the shop had icicles that drooped down from each letter.

We also wore long dark pants, and black-and-white with caps with googly eyes stuck to them.

'Could this get any more embarrassing?' I mumbled to myself.

Just then, a skinny man with dark hair handed me a pair of orange roller-skates. 'You're on the floor waiting tables.' His eyes then assessed Fletcher. 'And you're taking orders from the counter. Break time is in a few hours.' We stared at the man with blank expressions. 'Are you going to stand there? Go, go, go!'

As the man left, I realised that I had no idea how to roller-skate. This would be the longest, and most humiliating—wait, *one* of the most humiliating—moments of my life.

Fletcher pushed open the door to the kitchen, which was packed with staff members. Some made ice-cream at one end and prepared sundaes at the other.

When we stepped into the front part of the store, it was just as, or even more, chaotic. At the front of the store, a toddler used his spoon and threw ice-cream at the window. The toddler's mother apologised to the server that came with a wet cloth. A small group of kids gathered and the counter and screamed their orders to their parents. The parents were stressed as they chuckled.

Frosted-glass windows surrounded the area and gave the appearance that customers were inside an iceberg. The dining space was so large that it could fit a few living rooms in it. Tables, chairs and the booths that occupied the corners were all painted white. Pale light shone from ceiling, which used the same sort of glass as the windows. Goosebumps started to form along my arms from the air con that silently crept around the place; it felt like I was actually in Antarctica.

'Hey, new girl, I need another waiter today, not next Christmas!' a short, middle-aged woman shouted. Her black hair was in a bouffant style, secured with a white hairband.

I looked away from the front of the shop. 'Yep, right away!' I took my shoes off and stared around for a place to put them. The woman's head gestured behind me. There was a three-by-three shelf almost full up with pairs of shoes. One space was available. I put my shoes there and tied the laces on my skates.

After I washed my hands, she told me to head over to the counter and that she wasn't going to hold my hand the whole time. Sooner or later, I had to not be told everything to do.

I held my arms out so that I wouldn't fall over, at least that was my hope, and skated awkwardly to the counter. It was between the kitchen and the area where the register and a freezer, stocked with a variety of flavours of ice-cream and sorbets, stood.

Once I reached the counter, a man with mahogany-coloured skin called out from the kitchen. 'One order of Winter Witch Surprise for table seven.'

I picked the order up and skated with caution to where I had to go. It was hard to think about where Cassie had gone whilst I carried food. The order was shaped into a castle that had chocolate sauce oozing down the sides and was sprinkled with desiccated coconut. But I couldn't place what the flavour of the ice-cream was. When I thought that I'd gotten the hang of roller-skates, the bell by the front door rang and in walked my parents. They distracted me long enough that I lost my balance and dropped the ice-cream castle on the floor.

Embarrassment flooded through me. Shame froze my body in place. My parents couldn't go anywhere without being humiliated by me. We would always get ice-cream on Saturday. It wasn't a surprise to see them here. I swept the ruined dessert masterpiece back into the bowl and a hand rested on my shoulder. I looked up to find the man from the kitchen. He stood there with a mop and bucket in his hands.

'I'll clean this up. Go to the bathroom and wash your hands.' My eyes followed his gaze to where the toilets were located. As if he sensed that I felt like I had let him down, he said that it happened to everyone, even him on his first day.

I used the side of my body and opened the toilet door. The piston at the top of it hissed as the door closed behind me.

My hands were on the faucets when a voice whispered, *'Wipe that bit of ice-cream on your face.'*

The voice belonged to Lavinia, Mother Nature's

sister from a long time ago. She and I occupied the same body—mine. She chose me because of my strong will, and I wasn't the first person to be inhabited by Lavinia's spirit. The last was forced to create a woman with the power to see the future. I couldn't return to The Grotto anymore because Lavinia stole the powers that were meant for Rootha—Lavinia's sister—to give magic to disabled people. Rootha was angry by it, because the energy didn't belong to us; it belonged to their people. And that left me in the middle of this sisterly feud.

'Why?' I asked as I faced the mirror.

'Because it contains rose water.' I stared at her, still unsure what she was trying to tell me. 'Rose water is used for an elixir that changes your appearance to your heart's desire.'

Without a chance to think about it, Lavinia took control of my body and rubbed in a bit of the ice-cream on my face.

I looked away from the mirror for just a second. A tingling sensation travelled across my face. A moment later, I turned back to the tiny mirror to see my hair was longer, wavier and fawn in colour. It wasn't just my hair that changed, though—it was also the colour of my eyes.

They were green instead of brown. The rose water changed the way I looked.

The door flew open and the short woman appeared. She startled me. I knocked my wrist against the edge of the sink by accident.

'You all good, kid? What happened to your hair?'

'Oh, it was just a wig. My head was getting hot so I took it off.'

'Your wig reminds me of something I saw on the news.'

'Can't believe everything the news says.' The topic of the news made me uncomfortable.

'That's true.'

'Great, let's get back out there and make customers happy,' I blurted out as I rigidly marched out of the bathroom and the woman backed away from the door.

My parents waited for their order. Sadness filled their eyes as I saw a group of kids gossip about them. They must've seen the news. Imogen—Aiden's partner who helped him spread chaos throughout time—would believe that I didn't do anything to harm the person she considered a brother. I was too afraid to go back to the hospital with all the memories contained there.

The woman, who from her name tag was called Rita, crossed her arms in front of her chest and waited until the kids' attention was on her.

'This is not a place that tolerates bullying of any kind. Please leave.' She gestured her arm to the door.

'My mum, the mayor, will hear about this,' a girl with navy-blue braids declared.

'I'll be sure to pass that on when I see her tomorrow at my environmental committee gathering. A cause your mother is passionate about, yes?'

The girl's lips were pressed firm as she and her friends walked away.

Rita turned back to me. 'I hate bullies. Now, Peter

told me you weren't doing so well on the roller-skates earlier, so how would you like to handle the deliveries?'

Peter must've been that nice man from earlier.

'I can give it a go... wait, I don't have my licence.'

My fists clenched and unclenched themselves.

'Not to worry, all the deliveries are close by. You can use the bike out front. But your first delivery is to this couple.'

The couple was, in fact, my parents. How was I supposed to face them? What did they do to cope with the fact that I'm not home? And that the police wanted to ask me questions about a crime I didn't commit!

Rita handed me a folded paper bag. 'One...' I had to look at the label sideways to read their order. 'One litre tub of Boysenberry Dream to go.' They had ordered my favourite ice-cream flavour. My body broke down as a tidal wave of sadness threatened me to tell them that their daughter was right in front of them. I had to stand up straight and keep it together. They wouldn't have believed it was me with my new magical disguise.

'Thank you.' That was all my mum said as Dad led her to the exit.

'Well, I'd better get these deliveries started.' I turned away from Rita and scraped a hand under my eyes to wipe away the tears that had started to fall. Something clicked in my head. 'Where's the list of deliveries?'

'Peter just sent it to your phone from the app.'

'I, umm, lost my phone yesterday. I'm sorry.' In a

way, it felt like it was a half-lie I told.

'No need to apologise. Wait here and I'll print you a list, won't be long,' Rita said as she left through the kitchen.

I sat at an empty table and took in my surroundings. The booth to my left had two couples — one pair were boys, the other were girls. There were only two glasses of milkshakes that each couple seemed to be sharing. At the table directly to my right was a man typing on his laptop with a caramel milkshake and a bowl of cookies and cream that was slowly beginning to melt.

I turned to look behind me to see how Fletcher was doing. Rita then tapped me on my shoulder, her arm extended with a freezer bag on it. 'Here you go, I even included a clipboard for you, and your deliveries.'

'Thanks.'

'Once you've done those, you and your friend can call it a day.' She smiled.

'Thanks again.' I pushed the door open and found a yellow bicycle with a basket on the front to put all the items in. It was chained against the bike rack. Light from the lampposts flickered to life. The ice-cream-shaped clock said it was five-thirty in the afternoon. *How am I supposed to unlock the bike when I don't have a key?* I thought to myself.

Rita came back out again. Her forehead creased as if she'd forgotten something. She tossed me the key. Now I was ready to go. It then dawned on me that I didn't know how to ride a bike. Once I cleared my name, I had to make a list of things I wanted to do. So far, the imaginary list had roller-skating and that I needed to learn how to ride a bike.

Maybe if I learned now, it might clear my head of all my troubles—some of them, anyway.

I slipped on the helmet and knee and elbow pads that hung on the handlebars. The first place on the delivery list was the pet store, which was in the other direction of the electronics store. I didn't want to go in that direction. That was where I saw last night's news.

Where I became a criminal in the eyes of everyone who believed Georgina Church, the news anchor.

I flicked the kickstand up and felt the weight of the bike leaned one side. The bag was heavy. I wasn't going to be finished until after everyone went to bed. A lot of people craved some relief from this heat. I pulled the bike up, so it was level again. After a shaky start, I turned the bike in the other direction. The pathway was even and smooth; maybe this would be the easiest job I'd done today.

'How did you know that Turkish Delight had rose water in it?'

'When you've been on the Other Side as I have, you have the most fascinating conversations,' Lavinia answered.

'But that means...' I started.

'Yes, I had a conversation with the person who invented it.'

'Yeah, I got that.'

I hated to share my body with another spirit. It was hard enough deal with magical powers. Now there was even more pressure on myself.

The pet shop was on my right. It was half a metre to the entrance. The bike shook. At least it wasn't like before in the street over, where the bike's wheels ran over the tails of a group of cats—who scratched my face—which caused me to fall into a letterbox.

I crashed into the window next to the entrance, where an automatic door slid open to greet me. A neon sign buzzed above. I picked up the chain from the basket in front and tied the bike to the rack outside. Once inside, bag in hand, I was greeted by a guy whose dark fringe nearly covered his eyes.

'Hello, welcome to *Tails A' Waggin'*, where even our customers are wagging with excitement after they leave. How can I help you today?' he asked, his voice monotone.

'I'm here to deliver an order to...' I checked the list for the name. 'Eugene Pippins.'

'That's me,' the dark-haired guy replied. I also just happened to notice his orange shirt with a cat paw print stitched on it. It was in the same area as the company logo on my shirt.

'Okay, one two-point-five-litre tub of Strawberry Daydream, which you've already paid for,' I said while I repeated the order from the list.

After I gave him the pink tub of ice-cream, something caught my eye just behind the counter. A pair of rescued puppies, one white, the other black, tugged a toy at both ends.

I wish I had a puppy. Mum and Dad said a puppy was too expensive.

'Is there anything else I can help you with today?'

'No, that's it,' I said as my attention went back to him.

'Have a wag-a-riffic day,' he said, and I left the store.

After the *Tails A' Waggin'* order was checked off the list, the next delivery was at the dentist. So much for time to clear my head. I climbed back on the bike, and tried not to think about the were-creature that chased after me and Fletcher.

Nerves scraped against my ribs like branches that knocked against windows on a windy night.

When I arrived, there wasn't anyone at the front. The back was the exact same as the front—quiet. Giant portable spotlights stood guard outside. I heard voices on the inside, and walked up the to the back door. My eyes noticed the damaged railing from the were-creature's strength. It was strange to look at the dentist's office. Images from the night before with the scary beast shimmered past my eyes. What had the dentist thought when he got here this morning? Fletcher and I had tried to find a way to navigate the hallway in the dark; now I had to do it alone. Bright light from a torch blinded me. I threw up a hand to shield my eyes.

A woman with brunette hair tied in a plait came from around the corner at the end of the hall. The floor of the hallway had been covered with tiny holes and scratch marks, which were probably caused by the creature too.

She lowered her torch. 'Excuse me, but you can't be here. This is a crime scene.'

'I know, but someone ordered ice-cream, and I'm

here to deliver it to a…' I glanced down at the list. 'Tim Christie.'

A man in a head-to-toe protective suit came out from the room where Fletcher and I had hidden from the terrifying beast. 'That's me,' he announced. The woman shot him a fiery glare.

'You're not allowed to order food to an active crime scene. Do something wrong again and you'll be back at the academy.'

The tension in the air was so thick you could cut it with a butter knife.

'I'll eat it in the carpark, away from the action.'

She gestured to me to give him his ice-cream.

The last delivery was close to *The Chillin' Penguin*. It was a tan-coloured tub with pictures of cinnamon sticks on it, labelled *It's Chai'me to Relax*.

After his order was done, I jumped back on the bike and headed back to the ice-cream shop.

Then, once my foot flicked the kickstand down on the pavement, I went inside. Fletcher called me over from a table a couple of paces from the counter. As soon as I sat opposite him, Rita came and put a couple of sundaes in front of us.

'Not bad for your first day so far—you've earned these.'

'There isn't any chocolate in this, right?'

'Fletcher told me not to put any chocolate in yours,' Rita replied with a smile.

Fletcher had a strange look on his face. Rita shook her head a little. I was touched that Fletcher remembered that I didn't like chocolate. Then, she left us to talk amongst ourselves.

'So how was your day?' I asked as I picked up a spoon from the centre of the table where it sat with three more and some napkins.

'It was really fun. I got to serve ice-cream to everyone. Although I broke a few cones in the beginning.' He laughed as he recalled the events of his day. 'How did you go with your deliveries?'

'Would've liked to have gone to a different place that wasn't the dentist's office.'

'Oh, I guess that explains why you have a magical disguise on.'

'How did you know that?'

'Just a perk of being a Beta Voyant—being able to not only erase people's memories of magic but also able to see it too, I guess.' He scooped up a bit of his sundae and placed it happily in his mouth.

'Actually, this'—I circled my hand around my face—'was because my mum and dad were here.'

'Oh.'

'Yeah.'

Both of us sat in awkward silence as we finished our desserts. After that, Rita came back and asked us to take the rubbish out.

While she cleared away the table, Fletcher and I made our way to the back door where a couple of full bags of garbage waited for us. We each grabbed one and pushed the door open.

'How did we work a whole day and not find Cassie?' I yawned.

'Beats me. I don't have eyes at the back of my head,

like Mum claims she does,' Fletcher replied.

I threw open the lid to the dumpster. Fletcher and I took it in turns throwing in the bags.

Once that was shut, a piece of paper flew out and landed at my feet. There was no way I was going to pick it up.

'It's a receipt,' I said as my eyes studied the tiny print.

'It's from that Mexican takeaway place. Someone ordered the special, *La Fiesta* wrap,' Fletcher read from the docket. 'That wrap kinda sounds like the one Cassie gave you last year.'

'You think she's lying to us about her mum making it?' I asked.

Fletcher's eyes didn't look at mine, but to something behind.

I looked behind me and saw Cassie, her eyes wide with guilt.

A mix of emotions boiled in the pit of my stomach. I didn't know which one to follow.

Rage?

Sorrow?

Hurt?

Lavinia wanted me to choose rage. But I wanted to ask her why she would frame me for something I didn't do.

'Are you okay?' he asked.

I was about to answer, but Cassie ran away instead. My mind then chose which emotion to act on. I ran after her with Fletcher close behind me.

Cassie ran out of the alley toward the back of the ice-cream shop.

There was a tree with a thick trunk just ahead of her. It looked very old. I reached out with my arm and a branch snaked out and seized her by the waist. She struggled to break free from the tree's tight grip, but it was too strong for her. Fletcher and I stopped before the tree.

A couple walking their dog stood still. Curiosity appeared to overwhelm them. They looked between Cassie and me with wide eyes. Fletcher waved his hand in front of the couple. Magic the colour of forget-me-not blue rippled away from his fingers. When the ripples disappeared, the couple didn't know where they were. They walked back the other way, as they went about their day as though nothing ever happened.

I turned back to Cassie.

'Why did you run? I thought we were sisters?'

'You're no sister of mine,' she scoffed. 'And you're no sister of hers.'

As soon as she said that, her lips dried and cracked. Cassie's eyes widened as if she regretted the words she had said.

'Who are you talking about?' I asked.

My hand flew to Fletcher's bracelet. I drew power from it, then transferred that energy to her ankle.

Lavinia was in control now. Her hate drowned me as I tried to fight for control of my body.

She hovered my hand over her ankle. Just like her lips, her leg dried up too.

'What is she? Lavinia, if you can hear me, don't hurt her.'

Lavinia must've heard my thought. 'She's a golem. I know you know what it is.'

Since she shared my body, Lavinia knew I was a massive fantasy nerd.

Mother Nature's sister allowed me a brief moment of freedom to tell Fletcher what Cassie was.

How come I didn't see it before?

So, it was this replica that set me up?

Mother Nature must have the power to create golems, right?

'So, she's made from clay and answers to someone, and you two think that someone is Mother Nature,' Fletcher said, as he pieced together what I told him.

'And now this creature must pay for setting you up!' said Lavinia.

'Don't do it!' I turned around to see Rita behind us. 'Ana, I know you're in there.'

'How do you know my name?' I asked, shocked.

'It's Clara in disguise,' Fletcher replied.

This time it was me who was bewildered. 'How come you're just telling me now?'

'Clara told me not to earlier.'

3: A SHOCKING SURPRISE

'You're going to be a bundle of fun at parties, Fletcher,' Clara stated, who still looked like Rita from the ice-cream shop.

'Thank you, Clara.' He bowed gracefully.

'Ana, if you're in control, let Cassie go.'

'Not—until—she—pays—for—hurting—Ana.' Lavinia's rage sizzled through my body. I struggled for control.

Clara snapped her fingers. Red and blue strings of light removed her disguise. Her eyes glowed with the same colours as her magic for a second, until they returned to their usual shade of brown.

She then rocked back and forth on her feet. Lavinia felt distracted by this. Now was my chance to take my body back. I moved my right leg forward, then the left. The first few times I did this, it was as though I walked through quicksand.

When I reached Clara's side, she looked into my eyes and gave me a warm smile. 'I knew you had the strength to come back.' Clara swayed on her feet. I helped her to a bench.

'Ana, aren't you forgetting someone?'

My eyes wandered back to Cassie, who was still being held by the tree.

I flicked my wrist and she fell to the ground. When Lavinia possessed me and injured Cassie, it went against who I was. I never harmed people in that manner. A rush of guilt chilled my heart. Without even a 'thank you', she ran in the opposite direction from us.

'You think she'll tell Mother Nature?' Fletcher asked.

'I know she will. Which is why we have no time to waste.'

'What do you mean? How long have you been here?'

'I've been here secretly since I dropped the two of you off,' Clara explained.

'Why didn't you stay with us?' I asked.

'Just before I gave you those'—she pointed to our bracelets—'I remembered reading about a mirror that could, um...' Clara lost her train of thought. She stomped her foot in frustration.

Ever since she removed the magical lock from her spell book, Clara's memory of the portal spell had vanished, and now it appeared this consequence had affected her real-life memory too.

'It's okay, just take your time,' I explained to her, and placed a hand on her shoulder.

When I saw that Fletcher didn't copy me, I nudged his arm with my elbow. He followed my lead. Our bracelets glowed. This caught the attention of a few passersby.

'Let's head back inside,' said Clara, as she pushed herself hesitantly from the bench.

Back inside *The Chillin' Penguin*, there were still a few people that occupied tables and booths. A couple of women sat with their daughter in one of the booths, treating her to an ice-cream sundae. The little girl wore a gold medal around her neck. Her eyes grew with happiness at the giant treat. A guy played with his ice-cream with a spoon, a disappointed frown on his face, at a table nearby.

His eyes, along with everyone else's, turned in our direction. Some of them seemed fascinated by the glow of our bracelets.

'Mummy, can I get one?' a little girl squealed in delight at one of her dads.

'They look one of a kind, and very pricey,' the other dad replied.

The little girl slumped in her chair.

'Do you trust me?' Lavinia whispered to me.

'I don't think so,' I mumbled.

'I can help you to not draw any more attention, just please hear me out.'

'Like you drew attention outside earlier with Cassie?' I bit back.

'I just wanted to protect you, like I've done for centuries,' Lavinia explained.

I listened hesitantly to her.

'First, when someone brings Clara the orange sorbet she requested, you will have to create a dome. Also, tell Fletcher to make everyone forget about the glowing bracelets.'

'And what will the dome do?' I asked her.

'The dome will provide us with the illusion that we're just regular people talking about anything but magic. It also will allow us some privacy from everyone else's conversations,' Lavinia answered.

It was a great idea, since I hadn't thought of anything. Even if Lavinia forced me to hurt Cassie against my will, there could be spies that worked for Mother Nature.

I concentrated on Clara's snack, which had just been placed in front of her. It was a small, clear plastic bowl with three orange balls of sorbet and a metallic spoon. Light, the same colour as the dessert, shot up from the middle of it. The column of light then created the dome of silence and illusion that Lavinia said would protect us. Fletcher created a sphere of forget-me-not-blue-coloured energy between his hands. He released it, and then it phased through the dome to distract and erase everyone's magical memories. He told us that the sphere would go out once the job was done.

The three of us redirected our attention back to the bracelets, which still glowed. Blue and red lightning shot out of Clara's fingers and her dark-coloured wooden spell book appeared on the table. Together, our light washed over Clara's book. The combined light from the bracelets unlocked it. Clara opened it and flicked through the pages with great speed to find the part about a mirror that could help me.

Both beams of light danced across the blank pages of her book. Purple letters appeared on them. Relief blossomed on Clara's face. 'I knew I wasn't crazy. This is it!'

The light from the bracelets disappeared.

I read the top line aloud. 'The Mirror of Harmony.'

All of us read the passage to ourselves.

Things you will need:
Both halves of the mirror.
Coins from a wishing well.
The Fairy Supreme.

Once you have required what you need, climb to the top of the mountain of the place where the person whose body is being controlled presently calls home.

Then wait for the midday sun to melt the coins and the pieces of the mirror together. Only the Fairy Supreme can assemble the mirror.

'Once this mirror is complete, it will separate Lavinia from me.' I imagined the weight that would be lifted from my shoulders. No one would be able to control me ever again. It was as if I soaked in a nice, warm bath.

There was a sketch of what the mirror looked like after it was forged. It was oval-shaped with a delicate silver frame.

'Where do we find the Fairy Supreme?' Fletcher asked.

'You're supposed to start with the first thing on the list. Who told you otherwise?' Clara replied, a confused look on her face.

Fletcher shrugged his shoulders.

The lights flickered with a rapid pace like a heartbeat. I lost my concentration. The magic dome that surrounded us disappeared like sparklers that ran out of light.

Everyone stopped what they were doing. Most of us panicked. There hadn't been power outages since I'd arrived. The few that weren't panicking hadn't complained about the wi-fi being down.

Everything went dark.

The panic wasn't just inside the ice-cream shop. All the parents made eye contact with each other and understood each other. Together, all the families fled to the furthermost booth. It was behind where the three of us sat.

It carried on outside. People enjoying the evening raced to the nearest building like they were magnetised.

'What's happening?' I whispered. I didn't want to freak anyone out.

'Customers have been having electrical problems for a couple of days.'

Fletcher and I glanced at each other, and we had an idea. It could be something from when I altered the timeline.

'How did it happen?'

'I don't know, but the first complaint I can recall was from a nurse at the hospital.'

'Then what are we waiting for? Let's check it out!' Fletcher announced.

'What are you talking about? We have a mission,' I rebutted.

'This won't take long. I'm sure it's some kids pulling a prank,' Fletcher said. He didn't want to be right about our hunch.

He started to make his way towards the door.

I sighed as I followed him with Clara right behind me.

Another lot of people were arguing right in the

middle of the footpath about who had blocked the path first. People were frightened out here as well. This made it harder for us to keep up with Fletcher. On the other hand, Fletcher weaved through the crowds with ease like a summer breeze. Clara and I decided to pick up the pace.

After doing this for a few blocks, pain coursed through my thighs. I wanted to rest. When herds of people were about to run me over, Fletcher pulled me behind one of the pillars that stood outside the main entrance to the hospital.

'Hey, your disguise is gone,' Clara said. Worry grew across her face. Her concern transferred to me. Fletcher looked around then spotted a table with a box of disposable masks and gave one to me.

'I don't think this will fool anyone.'

'Just try and keep your head down.'

I rolled my eyes. 'What are we supposed to be looking out for anyway?'

'Something that's out of place,' Fletcher answered. His dark blue eyes glowed a forget-me-not-blue colour—the same shade of blue as his magic.

'That much I got, Captain Obvious. But I meant how do we know when...'

Fletcher pointed to a door with a red fire exit sign above it. The sign flickered just like the lights at *The Chillin' Penguin* and the rest of the town. 'There.'

The lights in the hospital were shut off. A symphony of panic and desperation filled the building. The sign above the door continued to blink with power.

Everyone around us turned on the torch function on their phones.

Light from a phone next to me shined right at my eyes. 'Hey, it's the girl from the news. The one everyone's after.'

It wasn't one light that pointed in my face anymore. The number of lights grew as people whispered about me. Glare reflected off the white walls and the landscape photos that hung there. I turned away from the light. My eyes tried to recover from it.

There wasn't much I could see, except darkness.

Something rolled under the toe of my shoe. With the help of the light that still followed behind me, I discovered that it was a dandelion. I picked it up and blew away the white stuff that covered the top of it. Nerves tickled my brain, as ideas came and went about how to escape from these angry patients.

A dark pink light embraced my hand and travelled to the plant.

I dropped it like it was on fire. Everyone's phones pointed in a new direction as the plant grew into a person. Glimpses of light caught the plant person's clothes—a green hoodie and jeans. The creature kept its arms folded in front of it. The crowd sighed in awe.

The three of us snuck away to another room.

We were halfway to the fire exit door when I bumped into someone. The person turned to see who had bumped her when the plant person sneezed and dandelion fluff filled the room.

'Hey, where did they go?'

It was the perfect distraction to approach the door

with no one paying attention to us. Fletcher sent blue sparkles in the air, to erase everyone's memories.

Clara pushed the door open to the basement. Since we were on the ground floor, it was an easy guess. We stared into darkness. Darkness stared back at us. A high-pitched noise squealed shut behind us. She must've let the door go. I waved my arm around until it landed on the cold metal railing and I shuffled myself towards the edge of the first step. Without any light, it was impossible to see how far down my foot had to go to reach the next stair.

The neon lights above flickered. They nearly gave me a heart attack. It was the unknown that scared me the most. *Who is down here? Why does anyone do this? Am I brave enough to face whatever or whoever is at the bottom of the stairs?* My thoughts weren't going to distract me. I had to find the first step. Once I did, I pushed through the fear that had simmered in the pit of my stomach.

A wicked cackle rose up from somewhere at the bottom of the stairs.

The laughter sparked something in my mind. 'I feel like I know that laugh?'

'Me too,' Fletcher whispered back.

'But how do I remember it?' Now my mind and my body were at war with each other.

Both tried to fight over who the winner would be.

We reached the bottom of the stairs. A whitish-blue glow throbbed ahead. It was beautiful and, at the same time, scary. Fletcher pushed past me, being braver than me—again.

'Hey, Ana,' he called back. His eyes didn't move from what was right in front of him

'Yeah?'

'I have a pretty good idea why that laugh was so familiar.'

Clara and I shuffled in right behind him. I pushed Fletcher over by accident.

'That's not possible.' We stared at the woman before us.

She hovered over a desk, on which sat a device that was torn apart. A rainbow of wires were exposed in a colourful mess, just like the woman's hair was the last time I saw her.

It was Professor Littleton. She was an assistant at the morgue, back in the fifties. She had been affected by magic, which caused her to go crazy. She also brought Charlotte, Elizabeth's—the current Mother Nature—daughter back to life. I turned Professor Littleton into a tree. *How is she a human again?* A tsunami of questions invaded my head.

She wore a lab coat with her name stitched onto the pocket just like the last time I saw her. But, this time, I noticed light brown specks of mould on it. The woman leaned over the table and studied the device before turning her attention to the cart behind her.

Clara took a few short breaths in She was about to sneeze. I tried to stop it—but it was too late.

'There's no use hiding. Insects do eventually get exterminated, you know,' spoke the woman.

Her dark green eyes caught us all from behind the door that was left ajar.

'She told me that you would find me sooner or later, Lavinia.'

'I'm not Lavinia!' I spat back.

'I know that, Anastasia. I'm not completely crazy, like *she* is.'

'Who is this *she* you're talking about?' I asked her. Shivers ran up my spine.

'Why don't you ask *her*?' The professor pointed to me.

I couldn't take all this. Both my hands went up to the sides of my head; I wanted to stop any more questions that built up in my mind.

'I believe this woman is talking about my sister,' Lavinia answered.

'But why would Mother Nature bring you back?' I turned back to the crazy professor, hands back down by my side.

'Because she understood what it's like to be competed against,' she replied. Her attention was focused on the machine that had been torn apart. There was a metallic rectangle that looked like some kind of battery, which was a little larger than the standard double or triple-A ones. A red jumper cable was attached to an old fuse box. The professor held the other clamp and one end of a black cable, which connected to the battery.

'And now what? You're going to prove to the world that you're *not* as crazy as a bowl of Fruit Swirlies?' Fletcher added.

'Typical boy, always underestimating a girl. No, actually, with the power I've borrowed from the town and also charging myself in the process...' White bolts of lightning swam around her fingers. 'I will make this defibrillator powerful enough to revive the dead.' *The energy that affected her must've warped how she wields magic.*

Professor Littleton's wrinkly fingers released both jumper cables. She then reassembled the old defibrillator that she had experimented on. Once that was done, the crazy professor flicked the switch on at the wall.

The device turned on. The screen lit up with all the things that a defibrillator had: heart rhythm, pulse, oxygen. Smoke sizzled out of the back of the small machine, filling the room and making us cough. Sparks jumped away from the machine. A small fire burned the defibrillator and sparks landed on shelves that sat above the device.

The blaze grew in size. The shelves were stocked with a variety of chemicals, which, since we were below a hospital, were flammable.

'Run!' I screamed and the three of us ran up back to the top of the stairs behind the fire exit sign that led us here. Where was Professor Littleton? Was she still in that small room? *Should I get her?* She was the reason we were in this mess. Would she report me to Mother Nature? I didn't want the Professor to think I was a monster, like the world already did.

Before I took a step down again, Clara grabbed my wrist. 'The smoke is too thick to breathe. She made her decision.'

I shrugged her hand free. 'There's got to be more time?' As the last word escaped my mouth, fire burned everything down there to a crisp. The flames climbed up the stairs now. After Clara dragged me out—before I could do my heroic act—Fletcher pushed the door shut.

4: A FAMILY MATTER

Fletcher and I sat at the bus station. There were too many people that had spotted me in Opal Creek. We had to get far away from here. Both of us were tired. While Clara got us our tickets to Cairns, it gave permission—although I didn't ask for it—for all these thoughts to rush around my head like a load of laundry through a tumble dryer. *Did Professor Littleton escape from the hospital basement? How are we going to get the first piece of this magic mirror?*

One of those questions were answered when the T.V. in the far-right corner flicked over to the local news. On the screen sat the woman who ruined my life. Georgina Church, the news anchor who read the evening news the night I was framed for something I didn't do. Her words still echoed in my head. Her flaming red hair was the only thing that stood out against the background beside her with the words:

FIRE AT LOCAL HOSPITAL

At the bottom of the screen, the captions read that I might have somehow been involved.

Anger boiled in the pit of my stomach. I wonder if Georgina thinks that any of her words can hurt people?

The rage continued to burn through my body. I was surprised that these tacky touristy sunglasses that Clara threw over my eyes didn't burn off.

I could feel the start of a storm in the air. Thunder whispered in my head. Hairs stood on the back of my neck and charcoal-grey clouds rolled in from all directions. The second that another journalist took over the screen was when I took a few deep breaths to calm myself down. The clouds vanished after that, and so did the sound of thunder in my head.

Another screen had a list that told passengers when the next bus was going to arrive. All the buses that headed north were highlighted in yellow; the ones that headed south were in blue. My eyes were focused on the yellow section. The next bus we had to catch was due to arrive in a couple of minutes.

After we raced back to Clara's apartment she rented as Rita, she told us that we had to leave as early as possible. My idea of early was five or six o'clock in the morning. Her idea of early was three o'clock in the morning. There should be a rule against being up that early.

I looked around the station and aside from the three of us and the guy at the front desk, there was one other person, who wore a hoodie with flames on it and dark jeans. Wouldn't that person have felt hot? Who wore a hoodie in summer?

A bus pulled out at the front of the station. Clara came back to me and Fletcher, who was snoring on my shoulder—it made me really uncomfortable. I didn't like being that close to people. She handed us our tickets as the man in the tiny office pressed a button in front of him and leaned over a small microphone.

'All pass-ugh-ngers heading north head to the...' The man yawned as he took a swig of the drink in front of him. '... front of the station now.' I shrugged the shoulder Fletcher was using as a pillow. After a couple of shakes, he woke with a sour look on his face.

'Come on, Fletcher, we're leaving. You can sleep on the bus,' Clara ordered.

The three of us—and the person in the hoodie—headed out to the front of the station.

There weren't a lot of us here. The atmosphere was dead quiet. Streetlights highlighted the bus shelter to my right with a bin next to it with a dreary yellow light. The dim lighting only just managed to illuminate the ginormous bus that stopped in front of us.

It was dark green with streaks of gold and white. There was an image of an emu with the words *Emu Bus Services* traced under it.

A short, old man with grey hair stepped out of the bus and walked over to us. He asked if any of us had any bags that needed to be stored in the baggage area. None of us did. With that, he climbed back up the stairs. The four of us approached the bus and the driver gestured for us to board the vehicle.

We all took our seats toward the back. Clara sat in front of Fletcher and me. The other person sat behind the three of us. After a few more minutes of waiting for anyone else to board, which there wasn't, the giant vehicle lurched forward for a second. The bus groaned in protest. The driver must've shifted the bus into the wrong gear, but after a few minutes, it ran smoother.

The streets of Opal Creek were completely empty. Who would be up at this hour anyway?

I peeked between the seats and saw the girl in the hoodie zoned out with a pair of green headphones on, until she saw that I stared at her.

'What?' she retaliated. Her rude reply made me jump in my seat a little.

'Nothing,' I answered, and turned back to face the back of the chair in front of me. The fabric that it was dressed in was something I'd seen on a bowling alley floor.

An electric hum pulsed throughout the bus. 'Good morning, passengers. My name is Len, and I will be your driver today. After we leave Opal Creek, it will be a nine-hour drive to Cairns, with a pit stop in Gin Gin.' The speaker became silent after his announcement.

I looked out the window as the bus drove its way through the streets and started to climb up a familiar hill. On the left, glimpses of the electronics store, ice-cream shop and the arcade passed by us. While on the right was the dentist's office was closer to the top of the hill. We passed the 'farewell' sign ten minutes later. An image of the mayor was plastered on it. She wore a polite grin—like a crescent moon. My experience in this town hadn't reflected her grin at all. It all started the day I got magic powers, then was thrown by a tree.

Now I was being hunted by the town for something

that never happened. The sky was pitch-black and starless; it made it impossible to tell if we passed the trees I remembered from the way into Opal Creek.

After another quick glance behind me to make sure that the girl didn't pay any attention to us, I tapped my bracelet with Fletcher's. Colourful light projected itself onto the back of the seat in front of me. My gaze drifted slightly to my shoulder, where a damp puddle of Fletcher's drool sat. I shifted my gaze over to his face. He continued drool.

I forced him off me and he almost hit his head on the window. He didn't seem bothered at all. 'Turn that light off!' he groaned and mumbled at the same time.

I ignored his complaint and continued to read. I didn't even know that I could access the information from Clara's book without the book in front me. It was like these bracelets had some kind of memory—kind of like a USB stick.

At some point, I must've fallen asleep. Someone nudged me. It was Fletcher. 'Hey, can you move? I need to go to the toilet.'

That was enough motivation I needed to move a bit quicker—since I still had to wake up. My eyes waited to adjust to the brightness outside. The bus didn't move. We must've been in Gin Gin. Sunlight pierced through the glass as I used the side of the seat in front of me to pull myself up so that Fletcher could get out. He still urged me to move. When I finally shuffled into the space where Clara sat, he raced out of the bus like he had ants in his pants.

Clara and I took our time getting out of the bus. She

seemed to have just woken up herself.

We stepped out of the vehicle and were greeted by the site of a two-storey building. It was hard to tell what it was—maybe a pub or a motel?

The building was made out of wood that had been worn down over time, like most of the buildings in Opal Creek. There weren't any cars on the street or even the locals, unless you counted the magpies that filled the silence with their voices.

The bus driver sat on a bench. 'I might just go splash some water on my face,' I told Clara as I approached him.

'Alright, I'll just stand here I guess,' Clara called from behind me.

'Excuse me.' The bus driver snapped back into reality when he heard my voice.

'Yes?' he answered.

'Do you know where the toilets are?'

'Just down the road a little bit.' He pointed in the opposite direction to where the bus was parked and towards a petrol station.

'Thanks.'

The driver waved at me as his way of saying 'You're welcome'.

As I walked along the silent street, it sent a chill over my skin. Something felt off. Luckily for me, I reached the service station faster than I thought. I pushed open the door to the girl's bathroom and saw the other passenger. She stood at one of the sinks that lined a wall of the restroom.

She stared at me as I stood at the sink next to her.

The girl's hair was pink and shaved on the sides of her head. The top of her hair seemed to be styled with some sort of curling gel through it.

The sink she used had been polluted with something black. There was a smoky scent that lingered in the air, but on further inspection it came from right next to me. I realised that she must've just washed soot from her hands. And sure enough, when my eyes glanced at her hands—they were as black as night.

'That's not a real human,' Lavinia said.

'How can you tell?' I wondered if Lavinia heard my question.

Lavinia took control of my body for a split second. I had no clue what she was thinking, until she made me look to the floor to see that her shoes were off. The water on the floor disappeared under her root-like feet. I took another look at her hands, and just like the other plants that Mother Nature turned into people, it was the same pale green complexion.

The air around us made my nerves tingle as it began to swirl everywhere. My arm reached up to grab the air, like a kite, and pulled it down. The air formed a bow and arrow.

'Who are you?' I asked. That was all I could get out before the spiritual barrier that separated Lavinia and I shut me out again. It was really hard to break through once she had taken control of my body.

'Your sister will never allow you to reassemble the mirror, Lavinia,' the girl answered. Her gaze still focused on the bathroom mirror. She then turned to face us. This might've been the most words this stranger had said the entire trip.

My curiosity helped me push through the barrier again. 'I'm Ana, not Lavinia. Please, just tell me why you don't want it assembled?'

'You and your companions are heading to the Daintree Rainforest. Are you not?'

The girl waved her hands in front of her and the soot that covered her hands rose into the air. Black fog began to surround the bathroom.

Lavinia took control again. 'Not so fast,' she cried out. My arm reached back and pulled an arrow of air from the quiver on my back. I sent it out toward the window just above us.

The window shattered and the dark cloud swam up toward it.

After Lavinia calmed down, I stormed out of the restroom and straight for where I left Clara.

Her brows pulled together. 'What's wrong?'

'You tell me.'

'What are you talking about?'

'One of Mother Nature's plant minions thinks that the first half of the mirror is in the Daintree Rainforest, also known as where Mother Nature forbids me to go!'

'I thought you knew?'

'At three o'clock in the morning? You think my brain is fully functioning when I have to be up before the crack of dawn?'

Fletcher headed toward us. He looked very relaxed, unlike when he had gotten off the bus. 'Hey, did I miss anything?'

'Just the fact that we're going to the place Mother Nature told me to stay away from.'

Clara sighed. 'When the mirror was destroyed, Mother Nature threw one half into the ocean, and the other isn't too far away from the first.'

'You couldn't have told us that before we got interrupted by Professor Littleton?'

'There wasn't much time.'

'There was too!'

'Okay, is everybody here?' the bus driver interrupted. He did a head count of the three of us, but was confused for a second. His eyes glanced at the clipboard in his hands. 'We seem to be missing a passenger. Where is Lily Pillson?'

'She told me she wasn't feeling well after the trip, so she called her family to pick her up.' The lie gracefully waltzed off my tongue. I didn't know I could do that until now. It was that or tell him the truth—that Lily was actually a plant that was sent by Mother Nature to prevent me from reassembling a mirror that could separate her sister's soul from my body.

We all boarded the bus. I sat by myself, so that I could calm down after the information that Clara had just dropped.

Before the bus took off, the driver put on a spy movie to keep us entertained. We continued our journey north. Exhaustion claimed me again. As the bus stopped hours later, at some point during the rest of the journey, I must've fallen asleep. When I opened my eyes, I was greeted by another bus next to me.

There was an image of a Ulysses butterfly—the symbol of Cairns—printed on the side.

'Hey, come on. Clara told me to come and get you. We have to get on another bus. The bus driver and Clara tried to wake you earlier, but you were fast asleep,' Fletcher said, lightly shaking me awake.

'Coming,' I groaned. My body swayed when I stood up. Fletcher didn't give me time to adjust my balance. He took my hand and almost hurled me out the door.

'About time; you can sleep through anything,' Clara greeted me after we stepped off the bus.

'Last call for anyone going to Kuranda,' called a light-blue-haired man. It was the same blue as both wings of the Ulysses.

The three of us ran over. My legs wobbled everywhere instead of placing one foot in front of the other. We managed to board the bus just as the man took his seat at the wheel. Fletcher and I sat in a pair of seats in the row across from Clara.

The bus left the depot a minute later. Along the way, we passed a council building made of steel and glass, rows of small department stores such as *Aim* and *Little M* and a city-like complex full of little cafes with ferns and multi-coloured flowers scattered around the area.

Further into the journey, we passed an army building and sugar cane fields.

Hazel eyes stared through the gap in our seats as a middle-aged Canadian couple surprised Fletcher and me. 'I'm sorry, I didn't mean to frighten you. What are you and your family going to go and see once we arrive? We're going to Bird World to see all the Aussie birds.' The woman who spoke wore an *I Love Australia* shirt. With excitement, she raised a camera that dangled from her neck.

Fletcher and I stared at each other and tried to search for an answer.

'We're going to the Butterfly Sanctuary,' Clara interrupted.

Disappointment was lightly etched in their eyes, before it was replaced by excitement. 'Oh, we went there last year. You'll love it!'

'I'm sure we will,' I answered.

The bus finally came to a slow halt. The area we stopped at was very quiet. The guy with the blue hair, whose name was Zac, said that usually the markets were on, except for Monday and Tuesday, which was today.

The town square was bordered by gift shops that were stocked with souvenirs and cafés with freshly baked treats. The town was a mirror image of the hinterlands back in Opal Creek—quiet and peaceful. At the centre was a little parkland where a bronze statue stood among a colourful variety of plants and the greenest grass I'd seen. Fletcher caught the smell of something being baked. He went around a corner and came back with a hot meat pie.

Meanwhile, I strolled over to one of the cafes—next to a souvenir shop that sold butterfly pendants and glassware in the shape of marine creatures—and ordered a croissant. Clara was the one who had to pay for lunch, and everything else due to my circumstance. She guided us back to where the bus was parked and then led us inside a butterfly aviary.

The gift shop was the first thing that welcomed us. As people walked through the door, all the butterflies were arranged in an arch around the sliding doors. I looked to my left and right. There were souvenirs everywhere, from butterfly umbrellas and jewellery, right down to t-shirts.

Once Clara paid for our entries to the aviary at the front desk—along with a pair of sunglasses with the Ulysses butterfly on the frames—we passed through a curtain of thick plastic strips, like at a butcher's shop.

'Here,' Clara said, as she passed me the sunglasses, 'just so you're not stuck with the one pair.' I made sure that nobody was looking in our direction before I changed part of my disguise.

After I pocketed the other pair of souvenir eyewear, it was easy to understand why no one paid any attention to us.

The enclosure was simply breathtaking. Butterflies and moths of different colours flitted around everywhere. A carved wood sign with bright colours that read *Fairy Garden* pointed to the far-right corner. Kids raced past me to get there. Natural light rained down throughout the entire aviary.

Clara used a sleight of hand to place a brochure of the facility in my hand. I opened it and there was a list of butterflies and moths, with their names and images of what they looked like. On the back was a picture of a target. Each of the rings had different colours. A yellow circle occupied the centre of it, followed by a ring of white, then finally one of pink. It was created so that butterflies could land on it.

I looked up and saw a clear glass dome that surrounded the place. It felt as if we were inside a really large terrarium. The sound of water dribbled down into a larger body, most likely a pond, which drew my attention away from the cloudless blue sky above. Ever since I was young, anything that involved water, from fountains to waves at the beach, always seemed to calm me down when I was stressed. I wished I had a camera so I could capture the beauty of this place. Lush, tropical plants surrounded us. Butterflies had landed on people that wore bright-coloured clothing. There was a blue one that sat on one lady's beige-coloured hat.

'Ana, over here,' Fletcher shouted. The people in the group that he and Clara had joined stared angrily at him, even Clara. He caved in on himself. 'Sorry,' he whispered to the group.

I climbed over a small wooden bridge to where he was.

One of the employees who worked there was about to explain about a flower called Shell Ginger. She pointed to it. The flower was made up of pale pink bell-shaped petals in a group just like grapes. On the inside of the petals were dashes of darker pink against a background of yellow.

A butterfly with black wings with splashes of white and yellow sat on the flower. The person who worked there called it a Birdswing butterfly, which was poisonous to birds. At least us humans were safe. Tiny craters decorated the footpath. When filled with water, these gave the insects a place to drink from.

When everyone looked in the opposite direction, Clara grabbed my hand and gestured that I grab Fletcher's. With her other hand, she touched one of the Shell Ginger's petals, and we were sucked up into the flower.

The next thing that we knew, we were in a forest. Unlike the butterfly aviary, there weren't as many flowers here. Right next to my foot was a small purple flower, which I saw on the family hike up the Emerald Mountains. My heart yearned to go back to that moment again.

I heard the sound of waves in the distance. It called to me, so I followed it. Trees with different-sized trunks tried to block my way to the ocean. The first thing I saw after I wrestled my way through the forest was the turquoise ocean. Purple light pulsed from the corner of my eye. It came from the bracelet. I looked backed and Fletcher's bracelet emitted an orange light.

What did this mean?

Something splashed in the sea. I didn't know what it was. All I saw was a pale brown fan shape that disappeared into the water.

A silver light appeared in the ocean. Seconds later, a girl waded toward us. I recognised this person from last year. Her name was Tara—a stonefish mermaid, and she packed a mean punch from what I remembered. *Or was it this year?* Our recent time travel had made time itself confusing. She wore the exact same emerald-green sari the last time I saw her.

Her knuckles were pale against her brown complexion. And her hair, black as the night sky, was woven into a plait. I tried to see the colour of her eyes, except she was distracted by the phone in her hands.

'Have we met?' I asked her.

She didn't answer.

'Hello?' Fletcher waved his hand in between the girl and her phone.

'Do you mind? I've almost got a new high score on *Cookie Crunch*,' the girl replied back as she slapped Fletcher's hand away from her view of her phone screen. Thankfully, she struck him with her palm, not the opposite side where the poisoned knuckles were. I remembered being hit with them last year and I managed to recover somehow—maybe it was Lavinia?

'Can you let us pass?' The bracelets must've picked up something. The only problem was Tara. She blocked the path to the ocean.

'No can do, girl with the awesome hair. Not until I hear from Mother Nature.'

'Please, we need what's out there.' I pointed to the ocean.

'I'm not going to believe your lies again, Lavinia,' a familiar voice answered.

I turned to where the voice was coming from.

There stood Mother Nature. I wasn't surprised to see her. I thought that maybe we could have snuck by without her knowledge.

Her dark hair was teased up into a beehive. She had

donned a flowy, dark blue, long-sleeved shirt with seashells printed on it. The white pants she wore were made from the same material as her top. This was also the first time I'd seen her barefoot.

'So *that* is why the bracelets are glowing, because part of the mirror is out there,' I said aloud.

'If only you were smart enough back then, you wouldn't have given the power away to total strangers,' Mother Nature bit back.

My fingers bent to form tight fists. 'I'm not Lavinia. I'm Ana. Why don't you believe me?'

'Because she's too stubborn to,' Lavinia whispered. Shock hit me in the face as I regained control back from Lavinia.

'You want to prove that my sister hasn't taken control of your body? Go and seek Morayna, and avoid using Lavinia for help. Only one of pure heart and mind can pass.'

'Come on, let's get this over with,' I called back to Clara and Fletcher. 'Fine then. Who is this Morayna and where can this person be found?'

'She lives at the bottom of an underwater cliff. Swim out to the edge of the reef and go all the way down to the bottom, where there isn't any light.'

'I'm coming too,' Fletcher said.

'No, my sister has to do this alone,' Mother Nature snapped. A determined smirk lifted one side of her mouth.

'Fletcher, I'll be fine,' I assured him and placed a kind hand on his arm.

'Good luck, Ana,' Fletcher said.

I smiled back at him as I waded into the sea. Once the water was past my waist, I took a deep breath and dove under the clear waves. *How am I supposed to hold my breath for that long?*

5: A TALE LONG FORGOTTEN

Every time I got closer to the edge of the reef, a strong current pushed me back. My arms started to burn up from exhaustion. Some of the fish around me faded away, and were replaced by images of merfolk. There were two mermen in particular that caught my eye: one had the tail of a clownfish, the other, a butterfly fish.

Both of their eyes were wide and their faces were pale.

I forced myself against the force of the current. Both mermen swam with haste, back and forth to the same places. A need to help dug its way up my stomach and into my heart. The current's power was like a really strong gust of wind.

My face was strained from the lack of air. I couldn't breathe underwater. I was desperate for air.

I gestured with my hands and tried to ask if they were okay. They just looked confused at each other.

The clownfish merman with wavy red hair blew a bubble, carried it and placed it over my head. I tried to shoo him away. I never liked it when total strangers invaded my space.

My mind spun out of control. *This isn't very hygienic.* My finger was just about to pop the bubble. The clownfish merman shook his head. All of a sudden, his facial expression became relaxed. He then breathed in and out. I repeated his actions. A huge sigh of relief flowed through my body and my cheeks weren't as tight.

I took my time to get my breath back. 'Are you okay?'

'No, we lost our daughter in the middle of an argument,' the red-haired merman replied.

'That's not the way I remember it,' the butterfly fish merman rebutted. His black hair danced through the motion of the current.

'You always say that.'

'Because it's true.'

Their argument was too much to keep up with. I could feel a headache about to happen.

'What does your daughter look like?'

'She's an octopus with blue string in her hair, to match the blue rings on her tentacles.'

While the yellow-tailed merman gave me a detailed description of their daughter, his partner got emotional and happy about something the other had said.

'It's funny, we never thought we'd become those parents who decided how to best identify our daughter so we wouldn't confuse her if there were kids like her, and now here we are.' The butterfly fish merman swam over to his emotional partner and pulled him into a hug.

'Oh, just before she left for school this morning I braided strings of pearls in her hair too,' the stripy-tailed merman added.

'That was a lovely idea, honey,' the dark-haired merman complimented him.

'Thank you,' the other merman answered, and his cheeks turned the same shade of red as his hair. 'Where shall we look first?'

'As in right now?' I asked.

'No time like the present.'

I had to find Morayna's hideout now; I couldn't look for their daughter. But I didn't want to hurt their feelings.

'Is something wrong?' asked the clownfish merman.

'It's just that I'm on my way to seek out Morayna, because she has something I need.'

'Morayna! I understand. I can't go with you to see her, she scares me.'

'Those stories are nothing but that—stories,' the butterfly fish merman stated.

'Can you stay with me please? In case she comes back?' The orange, white and black-finned merman suggested.

'Very well. Her name is Indigo, but we call her Indi for short. If she asks for her parents' names, tell her they are Archie'—the butterfly fish merman pointed to himself—'and Curtis.' He gestured to his partner.

'I will. How far is her cave?'

'Not far, just keep swimming straight, then dive down the edge of the reef,' Archie explained.

'Good luck on your quest. I hope you find what you seek,' the clownfish merman—Curtis—called back as I swam away, still fighting my way through the current.

My view of the reef was unlike the bright and

colourful wonder I had just left behind. There was only blue for as far as I could see. It was also difficult to tell the different types of coral because there wasn't any light down here. The temperature of the sea dropped the further I went out. A shiver rattled over my body. Jeans, a denim jacket and a t-shirt weren't the best clothes to keep out cold temperatures.

When I stared down at part of the reef that was swallowed in shadow, a faint gleam of something caught my attention. When I tried to find out what it was, my sore arms begged for me to take a break. There was a quest I had to finish first. My curiosity would have to wait, even though it screamed at me to investigate. It reminded me of the time when Mum told me to eat my vegetables before I could have one of her homemade chocolate chip cookies.

When I finally reached the edge of the reef, I had to force my painful arms to take me deeper. It seemed that my curiosity would get its wish, just not in the way it wanted. If it hadn't been for this bubble, I would've definitely had to have gone to the surface for air.

Sand and rock were all there was when I reached the bottom. There was a high chance that I could step on a stingray. My head looked up at shadows of sharks and other fish that swam by. At the very top, the water rippled in all directions.

I did make it all the way here, but now I had to figure out where Morayna lived. There were so many holes in the reef that it looked like Swiss cheese.

Which cave was Morayna's?

Something wiggled to my right. When I gazed in that direction, there was nothing there. I saw it again to my left.

'Try swimming straight ahead,' Lavinia suggested.

'You're the reason I'm in this mess.'

'Trust me.'

I ignored her advice, even though I swam toward that direction anyway. Once I passed through, I reached back and touched the place I came through. The illusion flickered as though heat rose from the road on a hot day. Above my head, the rest of the reef carried on with life. What they didn't know was that the illusion hid a dimly lit grotto.

There were all sorts of stuff thrown everywhere. Shelves made of sea rock surrounded most of the space. Books written by classical authors filled many of them. Another section of the shelves was taken over by jewellery. A crown made of paua shell caught my attention.

The space next to me shivered with movement. This time I knew I felt something, except nothing was there. Something wrapped around my shoulders. The end of a greenish-brown eel tail rested across them. My eyes followed it around to find a woman with thin, stretched-out skin. Her forehead creased with worry.

'Careful, that's one of a kind. The ship that it fell from should be around here somewhere, I think?' the eel woman said. Her jade-green eyes still fixed on me for another minute or so.

'Are you Morayna?'

'Why yes, I am. How did you hear of me?'

My mind went straight to the disagreement between the mermen I ran into earlier about the stories that people told. She must've seen the uncomfortable look on my face as I tried to think of an answer to her question.

'Ah, so you believe the stories about me being dangerous?'

'What? No. Yes. Maybe. I don't know. That wasn't my final answer. Mother Nature sent me here.'

'Relax, kid. I was only messing with you.' She swam over the top of me and stretched out on another net that looked like a hammock.

'We don't get many visitors here.' Her fingers fidgeted with a pair of pearl bracelets.

I looked around to find who else she talked about. There was only me and her there.

Morayna tilted her head down a touch. Next to me was a hermit crab that I had overlooked. The hermit crab stood there and blinked.

'Well, if Mother Nature sent you here, you must be after that, then.' The eel mermaid pointed one of her long, thin fingers to a piece of crystal opposite her. *Could that be part of the mirror?* 'Hamish, can you get that for me?'

When whoever she talked to didn't answer, I asked, 'Who's Hamish?'

'My assistant, of course. He's standing right next to you.' The hermit crab still didn't move.

'Looks like I've got to get it myself, again!'

Morayna pushed herself out of her hammock and swam over to the piece of crystal, which was about half the size of a computer tablet. She took it from the wall and was about to give it to me when she hesitated.

'Before I give this to you, you should know how I got it.'

'Oh, that's okay. I should probably get back...'

'Sit,' commanded Morayna.

I obeyed her and sat on the floor.

'Long ago, maybe centuries ago, Mother Nature summoned my ancestor to keep part of a mirror safe, and if anyone was to seek it other than her, or she had asked someone to collect it, she shouldn't give it to them. My ancestor honoured her agreement with Mother Nature of course. Then this got passed down through my family, and now, I have it.'

'And you don't know what it does?'

'Nope, but it's the worst mirror I've ever had. I can't see my reflection in it.'

'Because it's not an ordinary mirror. It reflects the image of the soul that has possessed its host,' Lavinia answered. The way she had answered Morayna's comment was rather rude and if Lavinia didn't share my body, I would've shoved her.

A thread of sunlight passed by the cave and gave the room a little light. I was about to leave when her tail wrapped around my leg. 'There is one thing that I just remembered: you need a fairy to help you make the mirror.'

'Um, I already knew that,' I answered, the pain in my limbs starting to return after my little rest.

'But did you know that you need the oldest fairy of

the time when you're going to make it?'

'The list just said the 'Fairy Supreme'. But that doesn't mean the oldest fairy?'

'It does, actually. You see, during the time those instructions were written, the Fairy Supreme was the oldest of the fairies.' Morayna unwound her tail from my leg.

I started to continue my way up to the surface, when the eel mermaid yelled, 'Remember to always believe in yourself. Don't let anyone else define who you are.' My head turned down to the cave. Morayna wrapped her woven shawl, which looked like it was made of strands of seaweed, around herself and headed back to her cave.

I'd only really met one fairy in my life, but Verona—the fairy who gave me and Fletcher enchanted jewellery to measure our friendship—couldn't be the *Fairy Supreme*, could she?

Out of the corner of my eye, there was that shining thing that caught my attention earlier. I thought it might've been the mirror piece, but I held it in my grasp; it must've been something else.

I attempted a one-handed duck dive down to the reef below, underwater. There wasn't much down there except for coral. When I reached the edge, however, I saw a figure with eight legs curled up on a rock. They had blue string and pearls that sometimes gleamed if light ever passed by.

'Are you Indi?' I asked the creature who cried under her crossed arms.

She pushed herself up from the rock and wiped her

face. 'Yeah, I am. Who are you?'

'My name is Ana. Your dads are worried about you.'

The lower half of Indi's body was orange with blue rings. 'Have they stopped fighting again?' She sniffled. 'They argue a lot. The kids at school say that because they copied a pair of fish that are enemies that that is the reason why they won't last as parents. So I stung them, and the principal sent me home. I didn't know what else to do. They have their good days too. Why does nobody get that?'

As Indi told me about her life and family, it sounded exactly like my current situation.

Then an idea zapped in my head.

'I've got to get back to the shore, and your home is on the way, how about I tell you my life? Maybe you could relate to it?'

She nodded. I held out my hand and she took it.

Along the way back to the beach, I told Indi about my life: how I lived in Perth before my family settled in Opal Creek, my new powers, the journey I was on last year. *Or should I say 'this year' now?* Time travel still confused me. Which led me to the story of how I now had another soul in my body and that Mother Nature didn't believe that I was me.

We reached the bright, colourful reef again. Merfolk took one glance at us and kept their children at a distance.

However, Archie and Curtis barged their way through the other merfolk and scooped Indi up. Our connected hands untangled as a result.

Indi's face lit up when her dads embraced her.

'Oh sweetheart, where did you go? We were so worried about you!' Curtis cried into his daughter's shoulder.

'I was at the edge of the reef,' Indi explained. Curtis's face was horrified by this. 'I know that you don't want me going out there, but I don't like it when you both argue.'

'We're sorry. Your father and I were talking about what's best for you. Truth is, we can't live without you,' Archie explained as her held tight to Curtis's hand.

'Well, luckily Ana found me and she told me that people aren't always going to understand me, that I have to believe like she's trying to do.'

Both mermer approached me.

'Thank you for finding our daughter. I made something for you. Creating things always calms my nerves.' Curtis held a pearl headband with a reddish-purple shell in the middle. He handed it to me.

'Thank you very much, it's beautiful.'

'To remember this moment, and to strive for hope.'

A tear grew at the corner of my eye. It fell down my face, and probably disappeared into the bubble that still surrounded my head.

The current whisked me away.

'Bye, I hope you never forget what I told you, Indi,' I shouted as the current pushed me further away from them.

'I won't. I hope to see you again soon,' she shouted back.

I watched as the three of them swam away. Bright

smiles expanded across their faces.

My body was scooped up by a wave that came from behind me. I had no control as I tossed and turned in its vortex. The bubble that kept my head dry popped the second my face was exposed to the ocean breeze, before my body continued to dance in the wave. A few seconds later, my body slid across the wet sand. It stopped inches before it touched a sandcastle with shells for windows.

'Ana. What happened? Did you get the mirror piece?' Fletcher asked as he and Clara helped me up from the ground. A cool breeze passed by me. It made my teeth chatter.

'I'm fine, thanks for asking,' I replied back. When both of them let go of my arms, I swayed with tiredness and collapsed on the sand again.

Clara helped me over to a rock to sit on. I was pretty sure it was the same rock that Cassie sat on last year when Fletcher, Cassie and I were carried here by Clara, for me to assist Charlotte in the Trial of Blood — a trial to become the next Water Guardian. The thought of Cassie stung my heart.

Five minutes passed by. It was enough time to get some fresh air. Mother Nature strode over to me. Her shirtsleeves and pant legs ruffled in the wind like the tails of a kite.

'Did you get the mirror piece?' she asked, her arms folded in front of her.

'I did.' I patted the shard of crystal that sat in my lap, which after another look, I realised was made of clear quartz.

'And you had no help from Lavinia?' Her eyes explored mine to find out the truth.

'Just for a second, but I ignored her,' I explained.

Mother Nature turned to the girl in the sari. 'Take the mirror piece from her.'

Tara had slowly started to approach me while her eyes were glued to her phone. Panic built up inside me. Mother Nature plucked the phone from her grasp.

'Hey!' Tara shouted. 'I just reached a new level.'

'You can have it back after you get that fragment of the mirror. NOW!'

Tara rolled her eyes. 'Fine.'

I stood atop the rock before Tara could grab the mirror, which was cradled in my arms. 'I did my best, what did you expect?'

'For you to trust yourself,' Mother Nature replied.

Tara waited for me at the rock. She was only a few steps away.

'Isn't that what I just did?' I protested. Mother Nature's eyebrows flew to the top of her head in anger.

Lavinia swapped places with me. 'Everything comes so easily to you, Rootha. You're the one no one can see anything wrong with, but I know better.'

Tara reached out and punched my ankle and swiped the fragment of quartz from my arms. Pain burned up my ankle when I fell from the rock. Just as she turned around, Lavinia touched her. My bracelet glowed at the same time.

I watched as her legs fused together and her tail returned. It was brown with spines that trailed down, the longest being closer to her tailbone. The shortest was just before her tail fanned out at the bottom.

She lay across the sand and groaned.

Mother Nature reached for the slice of crystal the same time we did.

The two of us—three if you counted souls—played tug of war with the part of the mirror.

'Why can't you admit that you lost?' Mother Nature growled.

'Because Anastasia was telling the truth. She did try her best, she even helped a lost sea creature child reunite with her parents,' Lavinia answered. 'I helped her to find Morayna's cave, and she did ignore me in the end.'

The poison took effect with every second that passed. My vision was blurry.

Mother Nature noticed that my body was weaker. She ripped the part of the mirror straight from my hands.

Victory covered her face as she walked away with her prize.

Fletcher and Clara were by my side. They dragged me across the beach.

It was the last thing I remembered before my world faded to black.

6: VERONA'S TRUTH

My eyes peeked open for a second. The sky was black as ink. Maybe I hadn't fully recovered from Tara's poison. *Was this a dream of some sort?* My eyelids flopped back down again.

'Are you okay?' Fletcher asked as he stood over me.

I thought that I was in a dream. Why would Fletcher be in my dream? Also, if I was in a dream, wouldn't I be comfortable? There were ridges pressing into my back. I looked down and found that I actually sat on a cobblestone path.

I forced my eyes open and sat bolt upright. The top half of my body swayed like a ship on the sea. 'What time is it?' I mumbled as my mouth stretched open and unleashed a yawn.

Fletcher pulled out his phone. A streetlight above him pulsed with warm light. The light from his phone highlighted his pale face even more. 'It's about five a.m. in Rome.'

'Rome!' I shouted. 'What are we doing in Rome?'

'We're here to find the Fairy Supreme,' Lavinia explained.

'Shouldn't we find the other half of the mirror? We already have...'

Memories flooded back to me like I was caught in the middle of a snowstorm.

Mother Nature had reclaimed the mirror fragment before I passed out from Tara's poisonous punch. This wouldn't have happened if I just lied and said nothing about Lavinia's suggestion. Defeat weighed heavy on my heart. The bitter feeling was about to consume me; it was about bring tears to my eyes. I paused. *This isn't like me. I'm not going to give up no matter how dark my thoughts become. I have to finish the quest, so I can get my life back.*

Behind me stood a sandstone wall that was the height of my forearm. The wall stretched around for a long distance until it stopped beside a group of statues. The light from the streetlights gave them a rough shape. The central statue stood out to me the most because he was familiar to me somehow. He looked like Neptune, God of the Sea. But it wasn't him, it was Oceanus, a Titan of the sea.

I realised now that we were gathered in front of the Trevi Fountain.

The sound of a camera lens made me turn to Fletcher. He had his phone out. 'The lighting is awful at this time of day.'

'Fletcher, is Ana awake yet?' Clara jogged over to us. 'You'll have to tell her the bad news.'

'What bad news?' I asked.

'Oh, you're awake. Are you, you?' Clara asked, startled that I had woken up. 'There aren't any restaurants or café's open until at least seven a.m.'

My stomach grumbled in protest.

'I'm sorry, but I didn't have much of a choice. Only a fairy knows where the wishing wells are located.'

'Why do we have to ask a fairy? Everyone knows where wishing wells are located. They can be found in a...' It was on the tip of my tongue, but somehow, I didn't know the answer.

Did someone erase a key memory from my mind?

A bold-red light glowed from a horse statue that sat below the one of the Titans. Verona phased through it. 'After the mirror was made, it was in the Fairy Supreme's best interest to erase the locations of the wishing wells from everyone's minds. Mother Nature sorted out Beta Voyants from every corner of the world to carry out this task. She didn't want anyone greedy enough to be overwhelmed by the power of wishing well coins.'

'But what reason could Mother Nature have had to do such a thing?' I asked.

'You all better follow me,' Verona instructed. Her feet touched the surface of the water. The tension of the water didn't break. We followed after her. All of our feet passed through the water and we landed in the fountain.

Verona chuckled to herself and disappeared through the horse statue again. The three of us copied her. The world around us vanished and was suddenly replaced by white light. It only lasted a few moments.

Once we passed through the portal, tall buildings made of the coins that the fairies' weapons were made from, equal parts majestic and intimidating, loomed above us. The ground had shallow lines etched into it.

Fletcher dragged me back as a tram-like cart full of coins zipped straight in front of me without warning.

Red light poured through every building.

'Welcome to the city of fairies. Today is a pretty normal day, unlike Valentine's Day, which is our busiest time of the year,' Verona announced.

'I thought that fairies only made weapons from coins?' I said, as I stared at the buildings.

'No, all of us divide the coins that are gathered in the Trevi. Some of it goes towards constructing our homes, and the rest goes to each fairy so we can create our weapons and armour.'

'What about the bridges that couples place love locks on? Are you planning on using those?' Fletcher asked.

'We have been considering it, now that the human governments have forbidden people from tossing coins in the fountain.'

'I've always wondered, doesn't melting the coins down into something new hurt the wish?'

'No, Anastasia. For you see, when you make a wish, you think that it's the coin that your wish goes out to, when in fact you're placing your wish in the universe,' Verona explained.

The ground was the only thing, except for the sky, that wasn't made of metal. Like the rest of Rome, it was made of cobblestones. We sat on the ledge of the fountain. Water poured out of the structure the moment we sat.

There was something different about this place. No one looked toward me with looks of disgust. None of the fairies seemed to alert any sort of authority figures. There was a calm energy to this place.

Clara noticed the relaxed look on my face. My shoulders loosened up, and my forehead wasn't wrinkled with frown lines. I settled into this calm state.

'Fairies judge people by what's in their hearts. They can sense that even though you have another spirit inside you, your heart is good.'

Verona nodded along. 'We live by our own rules. The rules of the heart.'

My body filled up with happiness. I hadn't felt like this since we returned from our journey through time. This place was where I felt most at home. When I thought of home, I thought about my parents and our brief meeting in the ice-cream shop. I tried to reign in my emotions, but it was too much. The tears marked my face with their tracks.

'About the wishing well, there is one in Opal Creek, but before you go you must know the full story.'

Verona explained to us that the Fairy Supreme before her, Orphelia, had made the mirror. When the mirror was destroyed, they didn't see that one of the First Peoples had seen the whole fight.

'When was this?' I asked.

'Around the fifteenth or sixteenth century.'

That was before the Europeans settled in Australia.

'What happened to Orphelia?' Fletcher asked.

'She fell under the spell of the wishing well coins, but back then there wasn't any such well around so Mother Nature built one, and kept it hidden from everyone but herself. That is why I won't help you reforge the mirror. I can't. I won't have history repeat itself.'

'But what if it doesn't?' I said desperately.

'Your heart doesn't believe the words you speak.'

'So, you *are* the Fairy Supreme?' Fletcher realised.

'Indeed, I am the oldest fairy. I was born in a city where one of the most tragic and beautiful love stories in literature took place, around the same time.'

'Verona.'

The fairy knew that I didn't mean her name, but the place she was born.

'Was there anything that could return Orphelia back to normal?'

Sadness clouded Verona's eyes. 'Unfortunately, no. Once she gave into the evil from the coins, no one could stop her until she ventured to the next part of her journey.'

'What do you mean 'evil'? Aren't all wishes good?' Fletcher asked.

'No. Before people make a wish, one that isn't of love, there is a darkness that surrounds them. This voice is like a siren—you may think it means well, but actually, it doesn't. That darkness lingers with the coin after the person has tossed it. Thankfully, we put a stop to people finding wishing wells.'

'I understand, but how can I free myself from Lavinia without putting you at risk?' Every voice that wasn't Lavinia's crowded my head with feelings of doubt.

Fletcher jumped up to his feet. 'Well, thank you

anyway, Verona. I'm sure we can think of something.' I could sense that Fletcher knew something that I didn't. He grabbed both Clara's and my hands and dragged us to the spot where the portal was.

'What are you doing?' I whispered to him.

'Thank you for understanding,' Verona said. She stared at the heart-shaped fountain.

'That's okaaaaayyyyyy,' I screamed. Fletcher pulled on my arm and it hurt. All of us disappeared into the portal.

We fell back into the fountain. The sun just peeked across the rooftops of the buildings and painted the sky in peach, yellow, orange and a touch of blue. A whistle pierced through the serene moment.

A small group of men and women in police uniforms blocked our path.

'It's the local police. RUN!' Clara alerted us.

Our clothes were soaked from our fall into the fountain. The icy wind attacked us. My teeth chattered crazily.

We ran up a small hill and ducked around a corner.

'What are you playing at, Fletcher?' I mumbled, so that no one but us could hear.

'Mother Nature may have hidden the locations of the wishing wells, right?'

'Yeah, and for good reason.'

'Everyone may not know where the wells are, except maybe one person. We need to go back to Opal Creek.' Fletcher waved his arm with the bracelet on it.

'You want to go against Verona's decision?' Clara answered.

'It wouldn't be the first time this has happened,' I told Clara.

'And how do you suggest we get back to Opal Creek? Lasso the nearest airplane?' Clara shouted in frustration at Fletcher.

Fletcher only smiled.

7: THE ORIGINS OF OPAL CREEK

'What if we put these back together? Could they give Clara her memories and magic back? If it works, we can get out of here before the police catch us,' Fletcher suggested as he gestured to the bracelets.

Clara and I looked at each other and thought that it wasn't a bad idea. She fished out the dark, wooden book.

The bracelets on our wrists glowed. Purple light highlighted the pages once again.

Fletcher was right, the information on the pages revealed themselves. Something felt different though. At first, the magic was calm. Now the magic was static and wild.

The magic jewellery on Fletcher's and my wrists snapped. They slithered up our arms, then leapt onto the book, which made the pages glow white. Clara hesitantly touched the cover. The light from the book deepened slightly to blue, the same blue that glowed from Fletcher's fingers when he used magic.

Clara gasped as the light flowed up to her head. Her dark eyes lit up with familiarity. She must've remembered something. Could it be that Clara knew how to make a portal again?

Fletcher's jaw was ajar.

Purple sparks twinkled from Clara's fingers. 'Let's get you home.'

Or back to the place that didn't feel like it anymore.

'Not what I thought would happen, but I'm so clever sometimes,' Fletcher said, crossing his arms in front of him. Pride glowed on his face.

Clara swirled her fingers in the palm of her hand. Purple lightning slithered around her fingers. It felt like a storm that began to brew.

Once she gathered enough energy, she threw it at the space in front of us. The portal started to twitch. 'Go. I don't know how long I can hold this.'

I was scared that I wasn't going to make it. Fletcher saw this in my face. He grabbed my hand and the two of us jumped through the portal.

Clara started to run for it right after we made it to the other side of the portal. The window between spaces shrunk the closer Clara got to it. She looked tired.

'I won't be able to make it through. When you restored my memory and my spell book, I lost my energy. I need time to recharge. It took a lot of energy to create a portal again, but the two of you can do this without me, I know you can.' She kept her eyes on me.

The portal disappeared.

'How are we supposed to find the well now?' I asked. Loneliness and hopelessness crashed through me like waves on the sea.

I can't do this without her. Where do we even start?

I should've jumped back through the portal to bring her back!

My arms hugged my folded legs as I sat down on the edge of a gutter. Someone came from behind me and rested a hand on my shoulder. Fletcher sat next to me.

'It's going to be okay,' he explained to me calmly as I slipped on the bucket hat that he took from the local convenience store.

Sadness chilled my bones and I was about to cover my eyes with the dark glasses when I turned to him. 'How can you be sure?'

'I'm not, but we have to think positive.'

I wiped my tears that gushed down my cheeks and inhaled. 'Where do we start then?'

Fletcher took a few minutes to observe our surroundings. He stared at the park in front of us. The sun had drained the lush green colour of the grass to a near brown. To the left stood the Emerald Mountains. From where we sat, we could see the rosella formation carved into each of the three peaks. The high school named its sports team after the beautiful bird. The water park resided in the opposite direction. School would start back shortly—that's what I thought, anyway. It had been hard to know what the date was with everything that'd happened in my life lately.

I was angry and sad that I wouldn't get a normal summer break like everyone else.

Fletcher glanced behind us where the school, the dentistry, the electronics store and many other stores were. He turned back to the park and just stared at it.

'We have to go to the council building,' he announced, as he jumped back up and offered me a hand. I grabbed it and stood up next to him. Fletcher pointed at the wall of trees. I narrowed my eyes at the tree line and saw glimpses of a pale building with Grecian columns, but it was hard to see any other features of the building from this far.

'Why do we have start there?' I asked.

Fletcher shrugged. 'No idea, but we won't get any answers standing here. Come on.'

With that, I followed him across the road to the park. We hopped over one of the wooden posts that bordered and separated the park from the rest of the town. There were so many people outside today.

A group of kids ran around and played a game of tag, while their parents watched from a giant picnic rug under the shade of a wattle tree—the yellow, round-shaped flowers looked like tiny pom-poms you'd find at the craft shop.

Further along, a few Aboriginal kids had their sketch pads out. Their eyes darted back and forth from their books to a bottlebrush tree with bold red flowers that resembled hair rollers.

'Ana, DUCK!' Fletcher warned me, but I was too late. A football knocked the hat from my head. I picked up the ball and handed it back to the boy who came over to apologise. He saw my hair and ran away with his ball. He must've seen me on the news. I scooped up the fallen bucket hat and quickly grabbed Fletcher's hat. We ran to the river past a gazebo where another family had a birthday party.

Fletcher pulled me to the left. I realised I had no idea where I was going.

We took a moment to catch our breath before we walked across a short bridge. Underneath it were rocks covered with a carpet of bright green moss. A trickle of water could be heard if the rhythm of my heart would slow down. The cool shade that surrounded us was a sweet relief from the harsh heat that we experienced not too long ago. There were even some ferns that dangled at the edge of the empty riverbank.

At the other end of the bridge were a few large steps made of dirt, the outline of each one traced by the roots of a pair of trees that guarded the exit. In the space between them stood the roof of the council building with the school logo on it. The shape of Australia in the colours of a white opal was painted just below it. There was a slight difference though — at the top of the symbol was a pale-headed rosella, just like the one carved into the mountains. A platypus with its duck-like bill lay underneath the bottom of the design.

I climbed my way up the makeshift stairs, and the trees helped me when I got a little off balance. Fletcher held his hand out to help me up the last step. I turned away from him to put my hat back on and made sure my sunnies were on too.

Fletcher continued to lead the way. It would be really easy to find him if I was ever lost, since he was the only redhead that I could see.

Before I came here, I researched a bit of what I

could find on the internet about Opal Creek. It turned out that further down the little stream was a freshwater creek rumoured to have a family of platypuses.

A strong scent of mashed potatoes lingered somewhere nearby. It made my stomach grumble so bad. I had completely lost track of what time it was when a bell tolled from the tower somewhere behind the main building.

'I really need to find some lunch fast,' I moaned to Fletcher as we strolled across the lawn, the savoury scent from earlier following as we did.

An elderly man with dark skin stood on a ladder with tins of paint lined across the rung above him. He dipped a brush into a tin of dark brown paint to touch up the platypus's body.

'Can you wait? We're almost there,' Fletcher answered.

'Almost where?' I whined back as someone bumped into me.

'I'm sorry, I should have watched…' both me and the person I bumped into said at the same time. Then we both laughed awkwardly as I helped the person gather up the papers that were knocked from her hands in the process.

The person's dark hair was tied into a ponytail. And she wore a green suit, the same shade as the plants we saw earlier. The colour stood out against her dark skin tone.

'Mayor Collinsford, I didn't realise it was you, I'm sorry.'

'That's okay. Have we met before?' she asked.

I chuckled. 'Oh, definitely not.'

Fletcher butted in. 'We're wondering if you could help us with a... school project.'

She looked down at her watch. 'I have a meeting to attend, and I'm five minutes late. What do you say we meet up in the café inside? Get whatever you want, my treat.'

'Well actually—' Fletcher started to say.

'We'd love to, thank you. That's very kind of you,' I swooped in and finished off his sentence.

She smiled as she ran off.

'What'd you do that for?' Fletcher whispered as the mayor power-walked away.

'Do you want to see me hangry?' I asked him.

'No,' Fletcher replied plainly.

A victorious smile filled me with pride. 'I'd knew you'd see it my way.' I pushed open one of the wooden doors and gestured for him to enter before me.

We waited for what must have been hours. We watched as people weaved in and out of different rooms. We also brainstormed ideas about how to locate the well, and came up empty. Each of the square tables had different-coloured Aboriginal paintings on them. Some had shades of blue in them, most of them had greens and browns. There was one table that was rectangular. It had part of a river that seemed to connect to ours. Was that just a coincidence, or was there something that linked the art on these table together?

I pushed my chair out with the backs of my knees. The chair ground against the concrete as I did. My head turned to the large table on my right and back to the one we sat at.

'What am I not seeing?' I muttered to myself.

The sound of a pair of high heels echoed behind me. 'It's pretty cool, isn't it?'

My brain worked overtime. I couldn't figure out what I was looking at. 'How do these all fit?'

'It's a map of the town. My dad painted them,' the mayor answered. She looked at our table. 'You haven't ordered anything yet?'

'We thought—' I looked over to Fletcher, who raised a brow at me, then back to Mayor Collinsford. 'I thought it would be rather strange to go up to tell the staff that we were with the mayor and no one would believe us.'

At that moment, the mayor burst out in laughter. 'You're a very sweet girl.' She approached the counter where the baked goods and coffee machine were and took a couple of menus for us. The mayor politely thanked the staff members and came back, each of her arms extended out to us with a list of food and drinks in each.

'What would you like to order?' the mayor asked.

Something lemony drifted our way. My stomach growled at me. It was like it told me to get whatever smelled so good.

'What's that scent?' I asked.

'That is my mum's famous lemon meringue pie with lemon myrtle.'

'I'll take one,' I declared.

'Slow down there, don't you want some proper lunch?' she chuckled.

'Can I get a ham, cheese and tomato sandwich?' I wanted something quick so that I could eat that amazing-scented treat.

'And for you?' The mayor's attention was on Fletcher.

'I'll just go for the club sandwich and the pie too, thanks.'

'You remind me of my brother when he was your age. He had a bottomless stomach. He ate so much food that I'm shocked he didn't eat our kitchen table.' The mayor giggled as she rose from her chair and walked back to the counter.

She waved to a woman who looked like the mayor, but older. She was probably the mayor's mother. The woman was busy in the kitchen.

After Mayor Collinsford placed our order at the front counter, she returned to us again and settled back into her seat. 'Now, what did you want to talk to me about?'

Fletcher and I looked at each other nervously.

'We want to know more about our town for our school project,' I explained.

'Well, the story goes that when my ancestors named this town, it was when my great, great, great, great...' The mayor looked up at the ceiling with a puzzled look. 'I think there are many more greats after that—grandmother saw a bright, opal-like structure being lowered into the ground. It was said that the structure was out of this world.'

My eyes widened with shock. I glanced over at Fletcher to see if he saw my reaction; thankfully he didn't.

Could she be describing that glowy thing I touched on the Archive wall at school last year? The thing that gave me visions of someone else's life? Could its location have something to do with the well? I thought to myself.

'That thing you touched last year was the vehicle that Rootha and I used to escape to the Surface, when we weren't supposed to,' Lavinia answered.

I slightly turned my attention away from the mayor and Fletcher.

'Don't interrupt my thoughts,' I muttered.

'Are you okay?' asked the mayor.

Too many answers to her question raced through my head like kites that battled strong breezes.

'You know when it feels like there are too many voices in your head?'

'Yes, I get them constantly,' Mayor Collinsford declared. There was a massive surge of relief in her answer.

I was so happy when Fletcher asked the question, 'What is the native name for Opal Creek?'

A sad expression clouded her face. 'Unfortunately, the tribe Elder is in a care facility and no one can fully understand her anymore.'

We lost our appetite after hearing the story.

'Well thank you for your help.' Fletcher extended his hand to the mayor. She accepted his gesture. I followed his action.

'Was there anything else I can help you with?'

'I think that's all for now,' Fletcher responded.

'If there's anything else, don't be scared to ask anytime.' The mayor smiled warmly as she walked away.

When she was a far enough distance away, Fletcher sent a pressed stare my way. 'What just happened?'

'Lavinia spoke to me. I hadn't heard from her in a while, but suddenly, she's back.'

'We will separate the two of you, whatever it takes. Did she say where to find that spaceship?'

My fingers dug deep into my palms as Lavinia screamed, *'It's not a SPACESHIP, child!'*

Both of my hands clutched my head. The echo from her scream bounced around my skull.

'What's up?' Fletcher asked.

'It's not a spaceship.'

'What isn't a spaceship?'

'The structure that's out of this world.'

'Then what is it?'

'It's an Earthshifter from the Florian race. A race of beings that dwelled underground long ago, until the day Rootha and I had our argument.'

'Are you saying that you and your sister are Florians?'

'What are you going on about?' Fletcher butted in.

'Yes.'

After Lavinia confirmed the truth about her and her sister, I didn't know how or what to do except just stand there with my mouth open.

Fletcher waved his hand in front of my face. 'Hello? Ana, what is it?'

'Lavinia and Mother Nature aren't from Earth,' I muttered.

'They're aliens!' Fletcher shouted excitedly.

'We're not aliens! Does he listen in his lessons?' Lavinia raised her voice again.

During our training—before the battle at Trevi Fountain—Mother Nature told us about where she came from. The first Mother Nature was a being known as a Florian. A pale-green-skinned species that dwelled in an underground society away from the world of humans above.

Until one day, someone dragged her up to the surface. They played amongst the trees or in the river. Then, Mother Nature gave her gifts to disabled people, and that was the last known account of the Florian race. I hadn't put together who the people were in the vision I had last year, until that very moment.

I pressed my lips into a thin line.

'Was it something I said?'

My eyebrows were raised in response to his question.

'So, where's the spa—' he started to say. 'I mean, whatever it's called?'

'It's an Earthshifter, and it's at school.'

'School?' Fletcher whined.

'Yes, more specifically, the Archives.'

'Specifically?'

'It just means that we need to focus on the Archives.'

'When should we go?'

I looked at him as if he asked me if space was cold.

'When the school is closed, Fletcher.'

'Cool, we get to break the rules.'

I'm glad one of us saw a positive in this situation. The idea of being a rule breaker made me sick to my stomach.

8: THE LOST WELL

The hardest part was to figure out how to occupy ourselves for the next few hours. Fletcher took me back to the arcade and the two of us were in a V.R. mystery game. Each level was set in a different location, from the Taj Mahal to a location where it *literally* felt like we were in Earth's orbit.

We were now in a witch's cottage, very different from Clara's set-up, when I looked up and saw the tiny, individual strings of the thatched roof. A shadow of a cat stretched across the rafters. Something similar to a potion bubbled close by.

A digital scroll that looked aged hovered between me and another witch with beige-coloured hair and skin. The witch waved at me. It had to be Fletcher, since he was the only other player in the game. When I raised my hands up to my eye level, warts sat on them.

Whoever made this game was going to hear from me.

The scroll unrolled itself to reveal a riddle written in cursive writing.

An ingredient is missing!
Can you find it by midnight before three?
Once you have added the missing ingredient, the kingdom will be free!

Once we had read it, the scroll vanished in a cloud of purple smoke. Fletcher and I stared cluelessly at each other. A white speech bubble appeared just behind Fletcher on the right. His eyes peered over my left shoulder. It instructed us to talk to the other witches in the coven, who were highlighted by a yellow glow. Each of the potion bottles glowed like those electronic memory games.

Before I could make up my mind where to start first, red light blared all around us. Another scroll popped up in front of us. It was a reminder about something with a codename: Operation Sneaky Sneak.

'Let's go, Ana,' Fletcher urged me as his avatar raised her arms, about to take something off her head, but there was nothing there. As soon as she did so, she disappeared. Fletcher must've removed his virtual reality helmet.

Someone then gently knocked on mine. It had to have been Fletcher. I unclipped the chin strap that held the helmet in place. Loud noises from all around me reminded me that we were in the arcade and not in a witch's cottage. Different shapes bounced across my eyes. They looked like tiny creatures under a microscope.

I saw Fletcher as he ran toward the door.

'Fletcher, hang on, buddy. Your friend has to let her eyes adjust to her surroundings,' Roxy advised.

Once my eyes were clear, Roxy's mouth hung open and her eyes filled with terror. She reached into the back pocket of her jeans and pulled out her phone and dialled a number. I realised Roxy hadn't seen my face since I avoided her gaze, except for now. 'Yes hello, police, I found the girl from the news. She's been staying in my arcade—you need to get down here now!'

'Roxy, NO! She didn't do what everyone thinks she did,' Fletcher pleaded. He ran back over and stood in between the two of us, his arms spread out to either side of him.

Roxy placed her hands on Fletcher's shoulders and looked him directly in his eyes.

'Fletcher, there are people in the world that may appear nice, but they behave differently on the inside.'

'Yes, I know. There's someone out there just like you described. And I'm staying by my friend's side because I know she isn't capable of doing what the *actual* person did on the news.'

He didn't wait for Roxy to answer as he pushed her hands from his shoulders, and grabbed my hand as we bolted through the door.

It felt like there were rainclouds inside me. They turned greyer the deeper I allowed my sadness to take over my body.

The purple clouds standing against the sky at sunset darkened and followed us, growing larger with every step we took. Roxy was about to walk out the door, so I summoned a gust of wind. It wrapped around my arm and it flicked the side door closed in front of her.

When we were out of the alleyway, everyone looked up from their phones. 'It's her!' a girl alerted the crowd.

They started to get closer to us. Rain spilled down from the clouds. Someone tried to push through the crowd that was gathering around us. I wouldn't allow anyone, except Fletcher, near me. I raised my wet hands in front of me. They glowed jade green.

Another person wormed their way amongst the crowd and slammed into the shield of rain I had just made. They tried to shove by, but nothing happened. My heart dropped as I looked up at the sky. The clouds had blocked out the sun now.

'Come on, Ana, I don't know how long your magic can hold them back,' Fletcher whispered.

'Neither do I,' I mumbled back.

I expanded the shield out to both sides of the street. It squeezed people closer together, so that no one could chase us. We made our way up the hill to the school. The pale green light around my hands twitched. My magic wasn't going to hold for much longer, but I willed myself to hang on.

When we arrived, our legs burned from the run up. A group of cleaners had just locked the gate at the front of the school.

My arms were super heavy from the weight of the rain shield. 'Is there another way around?'

A cheeky look grew across his face. 'Why find another way? This way is much more fun.'

'What way?' I asked.

Since there weren't any cars here, Fletcher ran across the road and leaped over the small chain-link fence. He turned around. 'Come on,' he yelled, 'your turn.'

I ground my teeth together. Fletcher could've alerted people where we were. My head turned left, then right, and back to the left again. There were no cars. I ran over the road like he did, but I stopped at the fence.

Sport wasn't something I was good at. I grabbed the fence with both hands, and climbed over like I was about to mount a horse. Fletcher looked at me weird. Once I was on the other side, he said that I could've jumped over it like he had. I just shrugged my shoulders.

We ran across the gum-covered pathway and passed the classrooms. This reminded me of my first day here. A set of doors blocked our path through the hallway, so Fletcher led me around building where the hallway was. Maybe fifty metres or so away was a shed where the groundskeeper kept his stuff.

We bolted past the library minutes later. Straight ahead was the performing arts building. A tall garden grew just before the entrance. Some of the plants were broken from people that had trampled through it.

After the drama building were the L.O.T.E. and art buildings. Just next to the music building sat the pair of paint-chipped doors that led to the Archives — where we researched about the people that I saw through a magical butterfly's wings. I wondered if we would encounter any more surprises? Fletcher grabbed the doors and shook them. They wouldn't move. No magical lock and key to help us this time.

'Allow me to be of assistance,' Lavinia offered.

I nodded, giving her permission to do what she

needed to. A trickle of energy channelled its way across my arm. My hands dug deeper into the wooden doors. Together, we pulled the doors apart as though they weren't locked. Darkness covered the stairs that stood on the other side. Fletcher fished his phone out of his pocket and a small light popped to life.

I stared at Fletcher and let out a short chuckle.

'What?' He held his phone in front of him.

Darkness surrounded us the second we passed the double doors. Fletcher and I stayed away from the walls after what happened last time—Cassie tried to squash a spider, but instead triggered the stairs that became a slide. If I remembered correctly, there should have been a light switch close by.

'How much battery do you have left on your phone?' I whispered into the dark space.

The light from Fletcher's phone went out.

'None now,' he said.

Déjà vu had struck again.

My arm reached for the switch. I hesitated for a second. What if someone noticed?

'You don't have to pull the switch if you don't want to,' Fletcher muttered from over my shoulder. 'By the way, what are we looking for?'

'The light from that wall I touched,' I answered while we walked through the corridor to the broken door.

'How are we going to get past the door this time?' Fletcher asked, as he leaned against the door. It creaked against his weight. He fell to the floor and a little laugh escaped me. Fletcher brushed himself off.

'I'm fine, all good. Just surprised me is all.'

We tiptoed into the room, just in case anyone was here. The shelves still needed to be cleaned. The temperature in here was a relief from the summer heat. Colourful lights jumped around from behind the last row of shelves and my nerves fizzled inside me for what I might see.

I reached out and touched the vibrant wall. Everything in the room vanished, including Fletcher, in a fog-like haze. Lavinia's worries overtook mine. Not only did my body share her soul, but I also figured out that it shared her memories, with the assistance of the opal-like piece in the wall.

Once again, my hands were my own. A man with brown hair with silver tips towered over me and the girl that stood next to him. Could she be Rootha? Her hair was tied into bun. She had the same colour hair as the man. He grasped a crystal lantern that radiated like the moon. This memory was more detailed and already longer than the last. I had no control over what I saw when I touched the shiny wall.

'Use the mirror, my daughter. Separate your sister's soul from this innocent child.'

A woman stood next to him with the same hair that I used to disguise myself back at the ice-cream shop, except the woman's hair was greyer. Her eyes overflowed with tears.

I struggled against two people dressed in brown-and-gold uniforms.

Rootha held up a mirror, the same one I needed to find.

'Please, stop. I'm not who you think I am!' I heard myself scream.

Deep down, there was an angry voice inside. I recognised this voice. It was the same one that shared my body.

I kicked the mirror out of Rootha's hand.

It hit the rock and cracked, shattering in two. The metal frame of the mirror rolled next to me. I used all my strength to throw the guards at the man and Rootha. They collapsed under the weight of the guards, all four of them in a heap I picked up the metallic piece of the mirror and ran.

My feet dug into the mountain as I climbed all the way to the top. I tossed the oval-shaped object into a well that was at the top of the mountain. You could see the entire place from there—I could get lost just as I stared out at the valley. Someone tackled me to the ground. I hit my head and saw a flower with only a few purple petals—it was the last thing I saw before I was back in the Archives with Fletcher.

'So, what did you see?' Fletcher's blue eyes sparkled with curiosity.

'I'm sorry you went through that.'

'The girl whose body I took over was never seen again,' Lavinia explained.

'What did you see?' Fletcher asked again.

'I know where to find the next part of the mirror.'

'That's great,' Fletcher shouted with excitement.

'Yeah, I guess it is.' A sad tone entered my voice. *How could her family have turned on Lavinia and that poor girl that way?* I still saw the memory in front of me. It would haunt me forever. Sadness drowned out everything else in my heart.

Hopefully for the last time today, we ran back down the hill, and we started to climb up the mountain. I had to stop a few steps up, though, as Fletcher yelled at me that he needed to rest for a bit. It wasn't until that moment that my legs felt stiff and a little bit cramped because I didn't stretch them before our journey.

I couldn't see how far down Fletcher was with the sun well and truly vanished from the horizon. A voice inside me screamed for me to rest, begged me to sit on the ground.

'You shall go no further, sister,' Mother Nature's voice called to me from a step above. A yellow glow appeared behind her, then quickly disappeared a second later.

'Couldn't you have waited until we had gotten to the well before telling me off… sister?' I said to her, my voice dripping with sarcasm.

'So, you admit that you have taken over this poor child's body?' There was an air of victory to her voice.

'Even I can tell that she's just kidding,' Fletcher explained.

Before she could respond, a purple light twisted in the air. Clara and Verona appeared and accidentally fell on top of Fletcher. I had to hide a giggle, although no one could see me in the early evening shade.

'I knew you would figure out a way to find the well. I hope we're not too late.' Verona saw that Mother Nature hovered over me like an angry teacher.

The light from the portal vanished.

'Since everyone's here, why don't we all head up to the well?' Clara said.

I ran over to hug her. Once I wrapped my arms around her, I noticed there was something different about her. She had long, wavy hair like Verona. Then it dawned on me that I had hugged Verona instead of Clara. It was difficult to tell who everyone was in the darkness.

A tidal wave of embarrassment sloshed through my stomach. I released her the second I started to feel unwell.

'Where are you, Clara?' I asked her.

She tapped me on the shoulder, which made me jump ten feet high. I turned around and squeezed her. I had missed her so much. She could tell that I did because she told me that I hugged her too tight. It didn't even occur to me that I did.

I unwound myself from her and wiped my arms under my eyes that had started to flow with tears. 'How did you manage to get back here?'

'You could've arrived a bit earlier,' Fletcher whispered.

I threw a cold glare in the direction of his voice.

'We would've been here sooner had it not been for the fact that I needed food and rest. I think I slept most of the time,' Clara explained.

'My grandma naps for most of the day too.'

Awkward silence echoed around us.

'Can we stay on topic, please? I will not allow you to go any further,' Mother Nature decreed.

'No, we were here first.'

'Watch your tongue.' Mother Nature's voice bubbled with anger.

I placed a hand on Fletcher's shoulder. 'Fletcher, it's okay—'

He shook my hand off. 'No, I'm not leaving until my friend is saved.'

Something struck my heart. This feeling of love had made me emotional. It was the first time that I'd felt like this since arriving in Opal Creek.

Both the necklaces and rings that Verona gave to Fletcher and me glowed a heavenly white light.

'How dare you speak to me with that tone?' Mother Nature called over to Fletcher, but he didn't seem to be hurt by her words.

I looked to Verona. A determined look froze her face. 'I will reforge the mirror.'

'No, I won't let another fairy risk her life again—that was the price paid last time,' rebutted Mother Nature.

'Even I can't ignore a pair of hearts destined to be together, it's Fairy Law.'

'Well, you can't reforge the mirror until midday anyway,' Mother Nature said.

'I might have a way around that,' Clara interrupted. Her eyes wandered over to me.

Something told me I wouldn't like her idea.

'Remember when we were in Scotland and you brought the sun from the other side of the world?'

My insides crumpled like paper at the very memory. I got in big trouble, and I didn't want to add to the pressure I felt.

Clara wove her way through our little group. The sound of her steps shuffled across the loose rocks of the mountain.

'How can you allow the mirror to be reforged again? Don't you feel the burden from what happened before?' Mother Nature asked Verona.

'Because the proof is before you, Mother Nature. Ana and Fletcher are true friends. I won't allow you to stand in the way of matters of the heart,' Verona explained. Coins jingled in a small pouch. Then they glowed in Verona's hands and transformed into a sword with two blades either side of the newly made hilt. The hilt glowed orange.

A sigh escaped Mother Nature's lips. 'Very well, I can't argue with Fairy Law. If anything happens like last time, it's on you, Clara.'

The uneasy tension continued to build as we climbed up the mountain. The sky had faded from indigo to pitch-black. A few stars lit the sky, which filled me with a little bit of hope.

'Hey, can we stop—' Fletcher started to ask.

My necklace glowed white again. 'Are you okay?'

His ring glowed, too, as he sat down. 'Nope. I feel sick. It's like I shouldn't be here.'

Before I could even ask the question of what was wrong with him, Mother Nature answered for me. 'It's the magic that surrounds the wishing wells. He has to untangle it to reveal the well, unless it's too difficult for him?'

'Why are you acting so un-Mother Naturely?'

Fletcher asked.

'Because the last fairy to forge the mirror lost her soul and we had to destroy her,' Verona explained. Fear cracked through her voice.

'Ana, can you come here please?' Clara asked from a distance away.

I placed a hand on Fletcher's shoulder, then walked over to where I heard her. 'Hey, Clara. Where are youuu—' The next step I took, I couldn't feel the ground under my foot. My heart dropped into the pit of my stomach.

'Woah, easy there, we don't want you going over the edge,' Clara said as she clenched her hand on the back of my shirt and pulled me away from the edge of the mountain.

We both fell to the ground. Shock rattled through me. I took deep and heavy breaths in and out.

'Thank you. The council should get some lights put in place,' I said to Clara. The grip I had on her arm was so tight that she had to pull my fingers away one at a time.

Blue light shone from behind me. I turned around and Fletcher had started to unravel the magic that hid the well. Blue threads of magic were tangled like they were in a ball of yarn.

Each time he tugged one strand free, a small knot formed on the other side. His face was strained. He stopped for a minute to catch his breath. I could sense that he pushed himself through this process. Fletcher's shoulders sagged with fatigue. *It must be something powerful for him to end up so tired.*

His eyes must've caught the worry that dwelled in mine. 'Lisa told me that unravelling something hidden was like unwrapping a present, but this is ridiculous.'

I chuckled to myself. Fletcher always made me laugh when situations were tense. I hoped he never lost that.

The magic that concealed the well had started to fall away like autumn leaves. The once smooth surface of the rock that Fletcher stood on revealed a small hole. I'd seen these around waterfalls. When I was in primary school, an Aboriginal woman told us that these were how they'd gather water.

I'd expected the well to be completely dried up, except I saw that it was full of water. It hadn't rained here for ages.

'When something is hidden, it looks as it did from the time it was sealed away,' Clara explained when she noticed the confusion on my face.

Fletcher's face was twisted with stress as he reversed the last of the enchantment on the well. Then he collapsed. I rushed over to him, but he waved me away with the little strength he had. He seemed fine, even though he looked as pale as a ghost.

'Now that that's done, you have to go down and get the mirror frame,' Mother Nature said.

'Can't Fletcher—' I was about to ask if he could come with me, but then I took it back when I saw how tired he looked. My body deflated with disappointment.

'How am I supposed to get down there?'

'Like this,' Mother Nature said. A green glow warmed her hand and she aimed it at me.

Lavinia was confused. 'How come when you told Ana and Fletcher about how their powers came to be, you said that Rootha passed her abilities to disabled children, when it was me who did that?'

'You always asked questions at weirdest times, Lavinia.'

Was it to hide the truth? Lavinia agreed with my theory, and had an idea.

'Next time, can you ask before you take over my body?' I muttered to her.

'You are still angry when she takes over without asking permission? I guess that's what happens when you don't do as you're told.'

Lavinia took over again. I'd give her a headache, if I could, every time she took over without asking. We conjured a lemon meringue pie from thin air and used it to teleport to the place that we weren't allowed to go to—Mother Nature's house. Lavinia had a mystery that needed to be solved and I was along for the ride.

9: AN EVIL HEART

Lavinia stormed the two of us up the makeshift stairs of Mother Nature's house. I caught glimpses of her windows and the table at the front.

Anger burned deep inside me. Lavinia never told me what she thought, unlike when she heard what I thought. All I knew was it had something to do with Mother Nature. Electricity buzzed down my arms. I clapped my hands together and a sphere of lightning rose from my palms. It gave the room some light, so it would be easier for me to see what Lavinia searched for.

We entered Mother Nature's bedroom. If she knew we were here, I'd get into more trouble, thanks to Lavinia and her hunch. After we passed through the doorway, on the left was a semi-circle impression on the wall. It was the other half of the mirror. *She gave one half to Morayna's ancestor and the second half had been here the whole time? How hadn't I noticed it until now?*

There was something in this room that felt off. I'd never felt it before, until now. A chill crawled up my spine. It came from an empty shelf that had been made from same sandstone as the house. A strong scent of sage lingered in the room, coming from a bundle that sat on a stone beside the bed, which had just been used. A thin mattress took over the large stone slab that she slept on. *She must be grumpy when she wakes up in the morning.*

We followed the off feeling back to the bookshelf. Something like a glitch shook before us.

It was as if all the negative emotions had rolled into one thing. We reached out to touch it when the glitch revealed a book—*Journal De Diaboli*—a book filled with dark magic that Professor Littleton had used to bring back Charlotte from the dead. That journal contained certain evil that a person could never come back from, which is why I avoided it.

The cover was brown and had a cracked, leather-like appearance. It looked like Clara's spell book but instead of the phases of the sun and moon, there were different colours of obsidian messily placed around the front cover and spine: mahogany, blue, black of course, green and rainbow—if you looked under the right light, that is. It was strange that this dreadful book wore the crystal that protected wearers against negativity.

'I knew it!' Lavinia shouted in victory. 'She thinks that I'm terrible for giving powers to disabled people, yet here she is using dark magic.'

'Just what do you think you're doing?' Mother Nature shouted as she appeared before us. I put the book back on the shelf without a second thought. The weight of the book was still heavy in my arm. A gross sensation oozed around my body.

'Proving that I was right. That you used dark magic to get your powers back, and you have the nerve to say that *I'm* the bad guy.'

Mother Nature was as still as a statue. She knew that Lavinia was right, but she didn't want to admit it.

'By the way, you can't get rid of dark magic with sage alone; you also need lavender.'

Clara waltzed into the room. 'What's going on here?' She stopped when she saw the dark magic book and turned to Mother Nature with a shocked expression. 'Why?'

A satisfied grin moved up my face. Lavinia enjoyed this. It was a moment when one sibling found out that the 'golden child' sibling wasn't as perfect as everyone thought.

Mother Nature pointed a finger to me, and her green eyes blazed with anger. 'I did it because of you.'

I pointed my own finger to my chest. 'What did I do?'

'You changed the timeline, for one thing. The last time I saw Charlotte was just before you and Fletcher returned.' Mother Nature's voice started to shake with sadness. 'We were having our weekly catch-ups in Rome when all of a sudden, she just vanished. Then these memories flooded my head of me going to the cemetery and leaving flowers for her.'

Guilt attacked me from the inside like I had swallowed pins and needles. 'I didn't mean to. I wanted her to live a normal, full life like everyone else.'

So, Lavinia's and my suspicions were correct. It was Mother Nature behind everything.

Fletcher marched forward and stopped in between me and Mother Nature. 'So, it was you who sent Ana's fake sister after her, and setting her up was, what, just the cherry on top?'

'And is there another reason?' Clara folded her arms.

'I knew you'd be coming back, Lavinia, so I did what I had to do to take back what's mine.'

'There are a group of people that needed to protect themselves against bullies.'

'And protecting your people wasn't good enough for you?' Mother Nature bit back.

'Why can't you see that there are other people aside from ours that need help?'

Mother Nature dug her fingers into her palms. 'Because we've been told to do just that, help our own kind.'

The ground shook beneath us.

'What's happening?' I asked.

'It's the consequences of using the Journal De Diaboli. It turns you into the thing that you hate,' Lavinia answered.

'Which is what, in her case?'

'I can't tell yet.'

'You know what, Lavinia, let's reforge the mirror. It will be so much easier for me to get angry with you,' Mother Nature shouted over the sound of the quake. She loosened her fists and headed in the direction of the tree that separated this world from the human one.

Another lemon meringue appeared before us.

Once we arrived back atop the mountain, Fletcher, Clara, Verona, Mother Nature and I stood around the hole where the well was.

'In order to reforge the mirror that can separate you and Lavinia from each other, you have to make it midday. Then, the sun can weld the mirror back together again. You did it when we were in Scotland, remember?' Clara explained.

'How could I forget?' The memory swirled to the front of my mind.

'Can't Verona just reforge the mirror with her magic?' Fletcher mumbled.

'No. This has to be done with the energy of the sun. Just like Mother Nature said I could easily be turned evil, like the Fairy Supreme before me,' Verona chimed in.

'Shouldn't I get all the mirror pieces first?' I asked.

'Yes,' Mother Nature's voice joined our conversation, 'because raising the sun takes a lot of energy, as you might remember?'

I tried to think back. The only thing I felt was shame. Clara and I had just met. She took me to Scotland and trained me in my magical abilities. She brought up the incident with Maggie and her friends, and it made me angry. After that, I parted the clouds, except instead I brought the sun forward. It was my first strike of many with Mother Nature.

Before I could answer Mother Nature, her hand glowed green again. She struck me with the light and I began to shrink. The shadows of the trees that were highlighted by moonlight became creepier the further I shrank. Being shorter than I usually was heightened my fear even more.

'What did you do that for?' My voice sounded

high-pitched.

I could imagine that Fletcher would be laughing at me.

'You have to go down into the well and get the pieces of the mirror frame.'

'How did they fit down there?'

'With magic.'

'But be careful, the well will whisper your darkest desires,' Verona warned me. A single star was reflected on the surface of the water, which gave me a spark of hope.

I waited to listen for anyone else's thoughts. When no one spoke, I reached my arms above my head to cover my ears and dove into the cool, dark well.

I couldn't remember the last time I went for a swim. If it wasn't for the whole crisis thing, I would've enjoyed this moment more. I didn't know why everyone was worried about the well—this was easy—until my hands scraped against a boulder. With me being the size of a USB, it was probably a rock that could fit in the palm of my hand at my normal height. A tiny grey cloud the size of a cotton ball covered the star, which was my only source of light.

'Aw, look how cute this cloud is,' Fletcher teased.

I pushed and pushed against the rock until my cheeks started to get sore. My hands brushed over the rock. It was stopping me from going any further. There was no way that I could have gotten through. I forgot to calm my heart rate beforehand. The energy that Lavinia granted me earlier came back, so I drew back my hand and struck the rock. When it cracked, the sound echoed loudly all around me. A trail of huge bubbles streamed out and tickled my face. It only lasted a second before I pushed and the rock snapped in two.

Siren-like voices whispered to me.

'I know you want to get even with the people who harmed you.'

It made me feel uneasy.

'You wanted the power for yourself, not your people.'

The pressure of those words weighed down on me from inside.

'It's not true,' Lavinia said.

'What's happening?' I asked myself.

'I don't know,' she replied.

I wish she would stop listening to my thoughts.

'You should punish your sister for using dark magic.' The voices became harder to shake off the deeper we dove. I hoped we would find the mirror frame soon.

Maybe Verona and Mother Nature were right—this was going to be harder than I thought.

My hand touched something cold and hard. It wasn't rock; it was metal. There were also tiny grooves that weren't quite melted into the frame. It reminded me of a coin. Now all I had to do was pull the frame out and reclaim the other half of the mirror. A little bit of pressure floated off my shoulders.

I moved my hand around the area where I had accidentally found the final piece. All I caught was the water that surrounded me. How could I find it again?

Frustrated, my arm swung out and smacked the

solid material of the mirror. I wasn't going to fail this time. My fingers wrapped around the sharp edge, and I tried to pull it free.

It didn't move.

How was I supposed to get it out from the bottom of this well?

My eyes started to drift closed. My arm loosened its grip from the frame. I wasn't doing this of my own free will. Something was wrong with me. Now my whole body had shut down due to lack of oxygen, and everything went blank.

Next thing I knew, I awoke at the top of the mountain again. Cold air nipped my wet body. Fletcher was next to me. He heaved his breaths in and out. Did he go for a run or something? I wasn't gone that long, was I?

'What happened?' I got up too quick and coughed up water.

'You blacked out underwater, so I rescued you, and got the mirror frame pieces out for you,' Fletcher explained.

'That's never happened to me before. Why would you risk your life, when you could've been at risk of giving in to your darkest desires? The frame is made of wishing well coins,' I said in the direction of his voice. It was still nighttime so it was hard to see where he was.

'Must I remind you again that we're friends, and friends would do anything for each other?' he answered. Despite the dark, I could picture the way he rolled his eyes.

'Let's get this over with so I can hold you responsible for putting our people at risk, Lavinia,' Mother Nature demanded.

A hand perched on my shoulder and I was a little scared. It was difficult for me to tell who people were when it was dark. The hand could've belonged to a stranger. The thought sent goosebumps over my arms.

'It's just me again,' Clara answered. 'When you're ready, I'll guide you through how to raise the sun, if you'd like?'

The memory of the time I did so still haunted me like a ghost. I placed both hands on the ground and slowly got up. My legs wobbled with unease. I hadn't rested much and my body didn't seem to want to work for a few moments.

I swayed on unsteady legs. A couple of people grabbed my arms tight. I closed my eyes and pictured the sun. Its bright and warm energy could not only help me see better, but it could also help warm my soaked body.

A yellow glow began to colour the inside of my closed eyes. I opened them and was blinded by the sun's strong light. It was hard to lift. Did it not want to rise into the sky because I was forcing it to rise earlier than usual? The energy was intense; it felt like I was lifting a huge tub of wet cement.

Even if I tried harder, I couldn't push it any further. The sky looked beautiful at sunrise. Peach, pale blue, yellow, orange and pink filled in what had been a black sky five minutes ago.

Dashes of mauve-coloured clouds hung in the sky. They looked like they were drawn with crayon. My hands dropped down to the sides of my body with fatigue. I collapsed to the ground.

'You have to keep going. The sun hasn't fully been raised yet.' Mother Nature stormed over to me. Her hair was a mess. The only way her hair could've gotten that way was if she had not long gotten out of bed. Anger crept into my body, but it was washed out by a tidal wave of tiredness.

'Can you at least grow the frame pieces back to its original size?' Clara sent Mother Nature a look so cold I felt frozen at the sight of it.

I stood up, legs shaking from not enough rest. 'I can try.'

'I know you will.' Clara's words comforted me as I turned in the direction of Mother Nature. She wasn't scared by the unwanted attention she got from me and covered her mouth as she yawned.

'All you have to do is point to the object that you want to grow and repeat it three times.'

"Grow. Grow. Grow'? Really?'

'Don't knock it 'til you try it. I used it a lot in my state fair's Community Largest Vegetable Contest. It received so many first place ribbons, also I was eight and couldn't stand waiting for it to naturally grow.' A proud grin pulled at Clara's cheeks.

'But won't I be at risk of being infected by the dark wishes?'

'Now that there isn't much water, you should be fine.'

My brows jumped into my hairline. '*Should* be fine?'

'Believe in yourself; you're stronger than you know.'

That was a lot of faith to have in someone who made a mistake that changed the timeline.

'You have me and Fletch—' Clara saw Fletcher asleep on the floor with his mouth wide open, like the clowns at the sideshow alley. 'You get the idea.'

I took a deep breath in, closed my eyes and tried to clear my mind of all the chaos, not just around me, but in my head too. 'Grow.' I opened one eye and saw the piece of metal expand from the size of a doll's accessory to the size of my hand. Green light dimmed from around my hands.

'Ah, ah, ah! No peeking,' Clara snapped at me.

I quickly closed my eye shut again. I didn't want to get on her bad side, like I was with pretty much everyone in the world. 'Grow,' I said again. Confidence jolted inside me. 'GROW!' I shouted with joy.

'That's enough,' Mother Nature said.

My body couldn't hold itself up any longer. I collapsed like a puppet whose strings had been cut. Everything went black after that.

Sunlight was the first thing I saw when I woke up. Fletcher was still asleep. I looked behind me and saw some sort of structure made entirely from logs that had an old look to them. There was something that hung from the top of the structure, a sort of clear, glass-like disc. I stretched my arms up and away from my body as I let out a yawn. One of my hands touched something hot. I pulled my hand away from it. It was a table shaped like an anvil, made from the same stone as the mountain.

'What's going on?' I asked. Was it warmer than when I went to sleep?

'Morning, sleepyhead. You've been asleep for seven hours.' Clara answered the question that was on my mind. 'I brought you some crepes for breakfast.'

The crepes had been placed on a paper plate with mixed berries, honey and icing sugar sprinkled on top. My stomach growled in happiness at the sight of the food.

'Did you get this from Paris?' I asked as Clara handed it to me.

'No, the market in town, actually.'

'Oh.' A bit of disappointment leaked its way out of my mouth.

'I needed to get away from all this.' She gestured her arms around the area around us.

'Mum—ss too early to get up, it's Saturday,' Fletcher moaned.

'Anyway, you woke just in time for Verona to reforge the mirror.'

'What do you mean?'

'When the sunlight goes through the crystal disc and onto the stone bench, the stone will get really hot. She'll place the metal pieces on it for it to be whole. After that, the same will be done with the mirror pieces. You'll be free of Lavinia once the two pieces are welded together again.'

My eyes wandered over to Verona. Her eyes filled with anxiety. I knew from previous conversations she didn't want history to repeat itself. She picked up the frame pieces first, just like Clara said. One at a time, Verona carefully set each part down on the stone table so that they both didn't overlap each other.

She jumped back like she had seen a giant snake when a strand of sunlight passed through the clear disc and drew a line along the line where the mirror had been broken. Dark smoke sizzled from the frame. It slithered toward Verona, but stopped as it was just about to touch her finger. The frame had become whole again.

The crystal pieces were next. Green strands of light circled around Mother Nature's hands. A mirror piece appeared in each hand. The one in her right hand had grains of sandstone around its edge. Mother Nature handed the pieces of quartz to Verona, who then placed them on the table, like she did with the broken frame.

The black smoke appeared again. It was thicker than before, and it crept up to Verona's heart before it disappeared.

Verona picked up the frame that she had put aside. Then she picked up the reflective mirror disc again. A dark smudge stained the purity of the clear stone. Verona blew on it, and the smudge disappeared. She placed the shiny disc into the bronze mirror frame. Two hair-like strands of smoke appeared this time. The trails of smoke started at one end of the newly reformed oval-shaped mirror and burned their way around the sides of the object until they joined back together at the other end.

They combined like two different colours of paint being mixed together. The eel-like tendril swam around Verona. She froze where she stood.

'Give in to your deepest desire—you know you want to,' it whispered darkly.

'Verona, don't listen to it!' Mother Nature cried as fear reflected in her eyes. *Did she recognise the voice?*

'I'm not going to be like her.' A tear escaped her eye. She must have thought about the last fairy to create the mirror.

'Of course not. You'll be better than her,' the dark voice comforted her.

The smoke shot up into a dark tornado. I tried to get close to it, but Clara pulled me back.

'If you touch that tornado, you'll turn evil.'

I didn't know. I had to do something to help Verona.

'That wouldn't be such a bad thing,' Mother Nature spat with bitterness, 'that way your true colours will be shown to everyone and prove that I'm the right person to be Mother Nature, not you.' She still must've thought that I was Lavinia.

The cloudless blue sky turned black for a single second. A scream erupted from inside the tornado. The smoky vortex disappeared and what remained was someone I didn't recognise.

A clump of hair sat behind the person. She had short, wavy hair with a bright green streak down the right side. Her toga was green too, with black circled around it. She wore bronze-coloured sandals on her feet. The figure turned around, and black swirled in her once loving green eyes.

It was Verona. She had given in.

She grabbed the pouch that was strung around her waist and emptied it, then welded the coins into her signature double-edged sword. Disgust filled her gaze.

'This weapon has poor craftsmanship.' Verona took the sword in both hands and snapped it like a twig. We were all shocked at the person before us. She stretched out her wings, and black smoke drifted away from them. 'I need to find a new weapon. See you around.'

She wiggled her fingers as she vanished before us.

10: ARTICLES FROM THE PAST

'So, now what do I do, sis?' Bitterness coated Mother Nature's tongue.

Guilt crept into my heart. It wasn't just Lavinia's, but mine as well. 'I thought that all would be okay, that history wouldn't repeat itself.'

Mother Nature crossed her arms in front of her. 'Well, it did. As usual I have to clean up your mess.'

Lavinia's spirit grew colder. 'I won't stand in your way.'

Her words didn't sound right to me. 'What? That's it? You're just going to give up, after everything we did?'

'Rootha's right. She'll take care of Verona.'

'No, there's got to be a way. There's always a way,' I said.

'If there was, it would be lost to the past,' Lavinia answered. Defeat had taken over her.

'I'm not going back, not after last time.' The memories of our last mission filled my head again.

Fletcher interrupted. 'Can one of you please tell me what you're talking about?'

'Going back to the past to find the answers we seek,' I explained to him.

'So, we have to bake another Key lime pie?' He

started to understand. Dread oozed out of him.

'You two will do no such thing. I'll handle this matter myself.' Mother Nature stood between me and Fletcher. She then pulled a lemon meringue pie out of her brown crocheted bag. I didn't really notice it amongst everything that had just happened. Mother Nature rotated her hand clockwise and a summery-yellow portal appeared.

'Yes, sister,' Lavinia obeyed. From all the time she had shared my body, this was the first time I'd felt her react like this, like she had given up. We watched as only Mother Nature stepped through the portal before its bright colour was dragged behind her.

'No, there's another way.' I walked over to the edge of the mountain and saw a building far away. A sign with two kids exchanging books sat atop it. It stood out a little more than the rest of the buildings in Opal Creek, which had nothing else like it.

'Isn't the library closed today?' Fletcher kneeled beside me. He crossed his fingers and begged.

'No, the library is open seven days a week. Come on, it's not going to attack you.'

'You don't know that for sure.'

'Then how did you find all those articles about those disabled people with powers?'

'Now I remember going there. I got distracted by the newest edition of *The Spectre*. I've been waiting weeks for it to come out.'

'I'll help you in any way I can,' Clara pitched in.

'Great, thanks Clara.' A warm sensation beamed in me.

After the three of us went back down the mountain, I had to help Fletcher back up after he fell on his bum several times. Lady Luck must've been on our side because the bus that took us back into town wasn't a long wait.

I managed to snag the window seat before Fletcher could. I looked out the window and saw the sun shine down on the summit. *We will fix this*, I thought, not only to myself, but to Lavinia too. She wouldn't be much help with Verona. I had to help her through it. My eyes tore themselves away from the view of the mountain and down to where I had clenched the Flo card in my hand so tight that parts of it turned a deep red. The material of the bus's seats were teal with brightly coloured shapes.

Clara grasped the lime green railing in front of her with every ounce of strength she had as the bus took a quick, sharp turn round a corner. It pulled to a stop at the station that the three of us were familiar with, but this time we were here at a decent time, sort of.

Hopefully, there wouldn't be any crazy plant person after me.

There was a rush of people that buzzed around us, possibly on their way to work. I hoped to have a job like everyone else soon. I yawned, then so did Fletcher. The sun's glare pushed through the cool temperature from the shade. I'd forgotten where I'd put my sunglasses.

Fletcher spotted a souvenir stand with sunglasses, along with copies of today's newspaper and magazines. He swiped a pair with Aboriginal art of the Peridot River on the frames.

These were my favourite pair that he had 'borrowed'. Clara tossed a five dollar note just behind the counter where a girl about my age nodded her head to music that echoed from her headphones. I was doing my best not to beat myself up about arriving back earlier than the time we had left.

'Which way is the library?' Fletcher asked.

'Shouldn't you know since you've lived here your whole life?' I replied.

He reached into his pocket and pulled out his phone. 'Yeah, well, Mum dropped me off, plus my memory isn't as great as yours.'

I looked over his shoulder as he typed in how to get to the library. We set off across the road. A few directions later, we came back to the bus station.

'Allow me, Fletcher,' Clara offered. She waved her hands in front of her and forget-me-not-blue shoeprints that matched Fletcher's appeared on the ground. 'I've cast a spell that allows us to follow the path you've taken to the library in the past.'

'Much better,' I sighed. Fletcher gazed in anger down at his phone.

We crossed the road like we did last time, but instead of doing a loop, we took the first right. An old information centre sat alone amongst the white wooden buildings with its red and yellow sign. I looked back and saw Fletcher's magic shoeprints disappear after he took a step forward. It was nice to have this moment of wonder with everything going on. We continued down this street and made a left.

The road that we turned onto was like the Nile River. The length of it overwhelmed me. However, I looked closer and saw that it was roughly divided into thirds. Fletcher ran to a confectionery shop where the man in the window rolled and chopped rainbow rock candy as an army of kids, each of them different heights, watched in fascination. Fletcher started to drool like he did on the bus.

Parents started to pull their kids away from the window, who cried out things like 'But I'm hungry' or 'Can't we stay a little longer please?' Some of the parents bought into their children's innocent acts; others told their children that they needed to grocery shopping otherwise they wouldn't eat tonight, or promised they'd come back another time. These interactions made me miss my parents.

After the kids left, I pulled Fletcher away from the window. It was like that time my dad tried to pull out my first loose tooth. 'Come on, Fletcher, let's go.' He wouldn't budge. I turned to Clara to see if she had any ideas. She snapped her fingers as one popped into her head.

'Hey, Fletcher, there's a doughnut shop down the road that's going to give a hundred dollars' worth of doughnuts to the person who can eat their signature *Boysenberry Explosion* doughnut the fastest.' Fletcher was interested, but needed more to convince him.

'It's a metre long,' I added.

A determined grin was on his face when he stared at us. 'Where is this place?'

The two of us led him along the road. He stared

hard at the other businesses as we walked on by.

Our trick worked, but for how much longer? Fletcher lifted his nose to the air like a bloodhound — sooner or later he'd find out that there wasn't a doughnut shop along this road. As luck had it, though, the library was a few metres away now. The pair of wooden doors that stood out the front of the building looked weathered and worn. Their colours were faded from age. *How come the council hasn't done anything about it?* Grime had even stained the section between the top of the front entrance and the roof. At least the image that I saw from the top of the mountain was in perfect condition.

We were about to cross the road when Fletcher grabbed Clara's and my arms at the same time. 'Hold up, there isn't any doughnut contest, is there?'

'Sorry, Fletcher, it was the only way for you to stay on track.'

He didn't seem to feel hurt by our scheme as a smile warmed his face. 'Nice job.' He pushed a closed hand toward me. I gave him a fist bump.

We crossed the road and entered the library, and someone held the door open for us as they were about to leave. 'Thank you,' I muttered in a deep voice. It was the only thing I could think of. I didn't know many people.

Our jaws hit the ground as we took in the weird claw machine that fetched customers' books. Fletcher didn't seem bored anymore. He dashed to one of the few electronic boards. I glanced over his shoulder to see an excited little girl, with twists that hung from her dark head, tap a selection of books.

The device came to life. 'I will get your choices right away, miss,' said the claw. It sped away from her and into the crowd of the other busy claw attachments. There were also librarians scattered among the shelves, filing the stacks of books cradled in their arms. It was a strange union between technology and humans.

To my right was a long and wide rectangular desk with desktop computers lined across both sides. A sign on a bookstand that promoted local author Tayla Forgetown said that the final book in her bestselling series was going to be available next week. It even promoted the book launch for the same day too. If I could clear my name, save Verona and myself by then, I would be able to go. She was one of my favourite authors.

Fletcher dragged me away from the stand. He was right; I had to stay on task. I placed a mental reminder to finish that series. The reality to clear my name was building up inside of me. I closed my eyes and took a few deep breaths. Anxiety throbbed in my veins. *Will I be able to save Verona before she has wreaked enough destruction that she can't come back from it? Will I be able to separate Lavinia and me in time?*

'Here we are.' Fletcher gestured to a desk. 'This was where I sat when I researched to see if there were any cases that were like yours the first time we met.' While Fletcher logged in, I took in more of the library. At the back was a section about the history of Opal Creek. It was the only section that technology didn't go to. Sunlight lit their clean wooden shelves. Brown-speckled boxes that used to be beige sat either at the top or bottom.

We had only just gotten here, and I was impatient already. The longer I was in public, the higher the chance someone might recognise me and report me to the police.

Fletcher waved the mouse next to the keyboard. 'Ah, here we go,' he said after he clicked on his browser history and found what he looking for.

He was on the local newspaper's website. It was an article from a few years ago of a blind man who surprised his wife with an anniversary trip to Venice. It was a harmless trip, except for the part where he teleported them right onto a gondola in broad daylight. The man, Herman Kettleby, explained to reporters at the time that he just thought it would be a nice thing for them to do, since he had started to lose his sight a few months prior.

'How come he awoke his powers just months after he started losing his eyesight but it took me twelve years to discover my powers?' I thought aloud. My eyes tried to remain focused on the article. A hint of jealousy crept into my soul. *Why didn't my powers emerge the day I was diagnosed with A.S.D?*

'We can't all learn the same way.' Fletcher's words helped ease my thoughts a little bit. I didn't know what I would do without a friend like him.

Fletcher opened a new tab and typed the man's name into the search bar and found that he was now a photographer that lived in Opal Creek with his wife.

In fact, he lived in the street on the opposite side of the library.

There was a timer on the screen to keep track of how long each person was allowed on the computer. Fletcher only had a minute left to log off so that someone else could use it.

'I wish we had more time,' I declared.

'Yeah, same; they're very strict when it comes to time limits on the computers. I was on here for half an hour longer than I was supposed to once, and got that time removed so that my next sessions were shorter,' Fletcher explained.

'How are we supposed to get the rest of the information we need?' Clara asked.

'Let's drop by my house. There are other articles than the ones I gave you.'

'Alright, Fletcher, time's up,' a woman with short, cinnamon-coloured hair said. 'While I love for kids to learn, you spent the longest time researching last time than I've ever seen you do.'

'It's because I'm here reading the comics,' he replied.

The woman looked around him and saw me and Clara behind him. 'Who are you? I've not seen Fletcher come here with friends before, only his brother, but that hasn't been for years now.'

Fletcher's eyes darkened with sadness when she mentioned Jesse—Fletcher's brother. The librarian's grey eyes took in my face. 'You look familiar. I could have sworn that I've seen you in the paper.'

My nerves tingled in my body. The breeze from

outside picked up in speed.

'We have to go, but it was nice to meet you,' Clara said, as Fletcher and I snuck by.

'Wait, you're that girl people are looking for.' The librarian's words stopped me in my tracks for a second. Everyone in the library then turned their attention to me. Before I let the voices in my head speak, Fletcher grabbed my hand and the three of us left the library as fast as we could.

A fruit and vegetable store stood next to the library.

'Quick, grab a tomato and throw it behind you,' Lavinia told me.

'Why?'

'No time for details, just do it.'

I grabbed the first tomato I saw. As soon as I touched it, the red flesh of the fruit glowed a beautiful teal colour. They were more expensive than the tomatoes Mum bought from the supermarket.

The person that tended the front counter yelled at me to pay for it. When I tossed it back, the tomato exploded into a cloud of fog.

'Where did that girl go?' one of the people from the library asked.

'Hey, watch it,' yelled another person.

While the crowd was distracted, we ran to Fletcher's house.

His garden was so vibrant and healthy, even through summer. A short frangipani tree sat in a purple pot right in front of the rhododendrons. I could hear their annoyed protests. Out of the new powers I had received, that was one of the top three weirdest. I wished there was someone else I could've talked to about everything, aside from Fletcher and Clara.

Two very excited dogs bounced up and down as if they were on trampolines. At least there were a few more friends. Fletcher walked over to his happy dogs. He opened the screen door and they raced toward me. I looked over to Clara, who was scared when one of the dogs jumped onto her legs.

'Are you okay, Clara?' Fletcher asked. 'Daisy, hop down, please.' The dog with the yellow collar did as she was told.

'She won't bite,' Fletcher explained. 'Just put your hand out and let her come to you.' He showed her how to do it, and Clara copied him. Daisy sniffed her hand, and seconds later, her little tousled head brushed against Clara's hand. She seemed more relaxed now.

'Is anyone home?' I squinted my eyes to see if I could see anyone else through the windows.

'No, Mum and Jesse are both at work. Wait here, and I'll be right back with the rest of the research.' Fletcher dashed back inside, as did Cam, his other dog with a light blue collar.

Daisy yipped at me to get my attention. I stared at her adorable dark eyes. I sat down and she leaped onto my lap, still happy to see me. There was a stick on the ground, so I picked it up and she bounced off me.

I slowly dragged the stick to the left, and she ran to the left. I pulled my arm the other way, and she followed like I held a treat. Then I threw the stick next door and yelled, 'Daisy, FETCH!' She ran after it.

I chuckled, until a car was about to turn into the driveway. There wasn't a place I could think to hide except in Fletcher's house. I brushed a hand across the worn railing and Clara followed after me as we scaled the few steps that led to his front door. Rust coated my hand in its sickly brown colour. I could sense the sickness as it climbed up my throat.

Fletcher came from around the corner as I threw the door open. Some of the rust coated the handle. I pressed my teeth together and cringed. The car had just pulled into the driveway.

'What's going on?' Fletcher asked, the manila folder in his hand.

'Someone's here! They can't see me, otherwise they'll turn me in. Get back in the house.' I panicked as I pushed him back inside.

The screen door hissed as it closed. I hope that person didn't see me.

Fletcher leaned around me to see who the person was. 'It's just my mum. We'll take care of her. You hide in my room—no one ever goes there,' he said with confidence.

Fletcher's mum opened the door the same time he opened his bedroom door and shoved me in. Both doors seemed to close at the same time.

'You're home early. Everything okay?' his mum, Marie, asked. 'Who are you?'

'Hi, Mrs McGregor, I'm Clara Wardell, one of Fletcher's teachers from school. I gave him a lift home; it was the least I could do for a prized student like

Fletcher here.' Clara's lie slid from her tongue without any fault.

'Yeah, school sent me home. I wasn't feeling well,' he explained.

His room hadn't changed a bit since I was over here last: his collection of comic books, his superhero bedspread, his vintage video game sleepwear and his beanbag, which I accidentally tripped over.

'What was that?' she asked. Fletcher's mum opened the door. I jumped back against the wall.

'Probably one of sculptures that grandma helped me decoupage fell off my shelf,' he chuckled. 'Probably should've sculpted the base so that it doesn't fall over.'

'While you do that, can you take your laundry with you? Or I could just put it on your bed,' she suggested. The door to Fletcher's room started to close again.

'It's okay, Mum, I'll sort it out.' The door stopped an inch before it met the doorframe.

'You said that last week.'

One of the dogs barked at the door.

'Daisy, you can't bring that inside,' Marie told her.

There was just enough room under his bed that I could hide under. Before I had the chance to see if I was right, Fletcher slipped inside. My body relaxed.

'You okay?' he asked. He walked over to his bed and dropped the pile of laundry on his bed.

'No. I'm still recovering from you almost giving me a heart attack.'

'Sorry about that.'

'That's okay.'

A knock echoed from Fletcher's door.

'Hey, Fletcher, come see this. There's something happening in Paris, something unusual. There's a girl on a bridge—she should probably find a new hairdresser. Here, let me show you, it's on my phone.

'I'll show him, if that's alright with you,' Clara offered.

'Okay…' Marie answered. Footsteps shuffled away from the door.

The door widened again. It was Clara, who slipped inside with Marie's phone in hand. The girl in the news report was an exact match to Verona. Her green and black toga stood her apart from everyone else. I thought I knew where the bridge was. I tried to picture it in my mind. As I did, a lemon meringue pie appeared before me. The juice and zest of the lemon levitated from the dessert. They danced around each other until a yellow light shined around the three of us. On the other side was the bridge. The citrus portal drew me in with a strong breeze. I grabbed a part of Fletcher's shirt and dragged him with me, without Clara.

11: A CHANGE OF HEARTS

Frozen wind scraped through the not-so-warm clothes that I wore as my teeth chattered. I hated the cold. I rubbed my hands angrily up and down the sides of my body. Fletcher copied me when he appeared on the bridge next to me. Another portal materialised and Clara stepped through without a care in the world.

'That's much better,' she sighed as she tugged on her warm puffer jacket that she just conjured.

'S-s-speak for yourself.' My teeth continued to rattle.

'Oh, right,' she chuckled.

Purple sparks snapped away from her fingers. Another spark of her magic popped in front of me from nowhere, and swirled around me.

My sneakers turned into thick snow boots, and I felt a few more layers being added to the top half of my body. The sleeves of my shirt grew longer down my arms, and even my jacket changed into something more suited for colder weather. I looked up at the dark sky as something lightweight and fluffy landed on my face. I brushed the beanie off my face and quickly pulled it over my head. Woollen gloves fit snug over my hands. My blue jeans were the only thing that seemed to remain as they were.

'Much better,' I sighed.

Police sirens screamed metres away from us. Blue light made it easier for us to know where to go. Clara changed Fletcher's outfit too. His teal puffer jacket almost blended into the police lights, and the black gloves that covered his hands made it seem he had none. His beanie matched the colour of his gloves.

The sound of the sirens scrambled my brain. It was difficult for me to concentrate on where we were.

'Any longer and we would have been popsicles,' Fletcher said as he smiled and hugged himself in his warmer clothes.

The three of us started to run across the bridge when, all of a sudden, our feet lifted off the wooden slabs.

Clara waved her hands and her magic rained down on us like snow. I couldn't feel the support of the ground underneath me anymore. I wasn't able to see that she had made us fly. *This is just like Peter Pan.*

'How are we supposed to get over there now?' I shouted. My nerves slithered throughout my body.

'You need to keep your voice down for one, and just pretend you're swimming.'

I did as Clara said. This reminded me of when Clara and I first met. I had had to put my trust in her when she phased me through a tree with her magic and the vines caught me on my way to the forest floor.

I pushed the air out of my way with each stroke forward. We had to find Verona before she could cause any damage. The light from the police cars pierced through the pearly white bulbs of the lampposts. The Pont des Arts bridge was different without its iconic love-padlocked fence.

'Weeee!' Fletcher let out an excited scream. 'Ana, you have to dive down, it's fun!'

I dove down and pushed my arms back as quick as I could. For a second, I felt like I was a comet that raced across the sky. The ground came closer to me than I realised.

'Fletcher! How do I stop?' I screamed.

'I can't remember exactly.'

'That's really helpful!'

I squeezed my eyes shut as I drifted inches away from the gloomy road, except that I didn't feel the thud of the ground under my feet. When I opened my eyes, one of Clara's hands glowed purple. I looked at my arms and they glowed the same colour as her hand. In fact, my whole body was covered in the magical light. The rapid beat of my heart began to slow down.

With Clara's help, the three of us managed to get to the place where the police lights were. Tall buildings with rows of paned windows and iron railings on the balconies surrounded us as we scaled our way up to a roof of one of the paved fortresses.

Pedestrian crossings were highlighted on the road. Verona stood in one of these streets. Her fists were clenched so tight that you could see the veins corded around her arms clear as day.

'Mademoiselle, please move out the way,' a workman said to her as calmly as he could. It didn't sound like it was the first time he had asked. Exhaustion breathed out of him with every word.

'You have something that I need,' Verona explained urgently.

'I don't think I do. Please move.' He waved his hand out of his truck.

She stalked closer to the man.

'What are you doing?' the man asked. His eyes widened as Verona walked toward him.

She tapped a finger on the man's arm and gestured to the back of the truck. 'Where are you taking these?'

'I'm to take them to an artist not far away from here,' he said. The workman's French accent sounded the complete opposite from his earlier comment. He must have been put under a spell when Verona touched him.

'Hmm, an artist? Take me to him now!' she ordered.

The man got out of his car, took her hand and led her around to the passenger side of his truck. He opened the door for her as she climbed up. The shredded skirt of her dress almost got caught in the door when it closed.

'Watch it!' Verona spat at the workman.

'I'm sorry, mistress.'

'You should be. Now take me to this *artist*,' she ordered as she fixed her hair to make it more presentable.

The truck rumbled forward until long, metallic vines leaned forward and dug themselves into the back of the truck. The tyres screeched against the road.

Little grey clouds of smoke sizzled up from the ground.

Where did those come from?

I followed the metallic lines away from the truck to the lampposts that lit up the streets. There was just enough light to see what the truck carried. Locks of different colours and shapes peeked out from the holes that pierced the vehicle.

'*She's here,*' Lavinia whispered to me. Fear overcame her.

'Who are you talking about?'

'What did she say?' Fletcher asked.

I was about to answer his question when another tendril from a lamppost lunged at Verona the second she got out of the truck and held her in a tight hug. She couldn't escape its firm squeeze, no matter how many times she tried.

'Glad to see you're getting your hands dirty yourself, instead of relying on other people,' Verona said uncomfortably.

Mother Nature took a few steps out from a nearby dark alley and into the warm and eerie light. Her hair had no accessories; it just hung down the brown trench coat that covered her black catsuit, which had silhouettes of leafless trees.

'When my sister gets into trouble, I have to clean up her mess.' She burned an annoyed stare into my eyes.

I was about to say something, but Lavinia didn't allow me to speak.

'*No, she's right. This is all my fault. Let her handle this,*' she ordered me. I turned around from the rooftop that the three of us squatted on. I accidentally leaned too far forward and a flowerpot smashed to the ground.

I glanced behind me. Mother Nature had flown up to the top of the building. She had an amused expression. 'It took you years to finally have the guts to fix your mistakes.' There was something different about her. The Mother Nature I first met had looked young and ethereal. Her hands started to shake. It wasn't from the cold but something else.

'She's used Journal De Diaboli to gain the power that I gave away. Except that if anyone uses the book just once, it'll turn them into the thing they hate.'

An angry blue heat burned along the metal bars that restrained Verona. She picked up the melted pieces of the lamppost then hugged the object that kept her prisoner.

The black metal brightened in the same blue as before. Glass shattered and rained down around her into particles as fine as sand. Sparks of electricity danced dangerously around her. The heat didn't seem to bother her, even though the skin all across her arms and the left side of her face was badly burned and blistered.

The reddish splotches on her skin healed quickly. 'Is that the best you've got, Mother Nature?' All that was left of the charming lamppost was a blob of metal. With the broken pieces, Verona leaped on top of the truck and carved open the back of it.

She jumped into the hole and came out with as many locks as she could carry.

Verona dropped them in front of her and turned the colourful group of metal into the copperish colour of pennies.

Lavinia had loosened her hold over me. I guess when she tried to not let me speak and move, she became more tired.

The lights from inside the buildings around us flicked on like popcorn being cooked as people peeked through their curtains.

Verona's hands were covered in blue light. She pulled a metallic bar away from the mound of locks in front of her. Then, she braided the metal into a staff. Verona ripped other love tokens from the fence and melted it in her hands. She created a scythe-like blade with the hot liquid copper from the clasps of affection.

Now was our moment to strike. The three of us dropped from our hiding place and the purple glow that surrounded us disappeared.

When she was finished, Verona jumped back into the cab of the truck to get more love locks. Small groups, mostly couples, appeared out of some of the buildings. Flecks of bright green glowed in their eyes. She tossed broken pieces of metal from the fence aside.

A newly forged scythe glimmered in her hand. 'Follow me, my friends. Let us gather our numbers and plan our next attack.' A wicked light burned in Verona's eyes. She turned back to the workman as she flipped back to the truck and patched over the holes that pierced it with her hands.

'Oh, look, company. At least you won't be alone. Lock them all up in there.' Verona pointed back to the truck container.

'With what, mistress?' asked the zombified workman.

She picked up the bits of metal she threw away earlier. 'Use these. Once you've done that, I will transport you.'

With her new followers, Verona disappeared into a web of smoke. Her first follower tapped me, Clara, Fletcher and Mother Nature with the bits of the fallen lamppost. As soon as the metal touched us, it took on a life of its own and squeezed around us, then the workman carried us into the truck and locked us inside. The sound of his footsteps faded away.

12: PHOTOS THAT TELL A STORY

We were trapped in total darkness with no room to move. Footsteps echoed across to the other side of the truck. 'Are you happy now? You let her get away,' Mother Nature yelled. I wished my hands were free so I could cover my ears. Her shouts were louder in this enclosed space.

'She's not Lavinia,' Clara explained. From what I could hear, Clara was closest to one of the sides of the truck.

'You have been with her for too long. She's twisted your mind, Clara,' Mother Nature decreed.

Fear tickled my body as a slight wind whispered around us.

'She hasn't. You're the one who's twisted, using dark magic to restore your powers so that you can claim hers.'

Anxiety rustled through me as the breeze picked up. I wanted them to stop this fight.

'They were never hers to begin with—'

'STOP FIGHTING!' I yelled. The wind outside now rocked the vehicle angrily. Thunder clapped from above and struck the roof.

I tried again. Frustration charged itself around my arms. Blue-white sparks of lightning weaved around my fingers. I summoned a bolt of lightning, which landed on the roof of the trailer. A tiny hole sizzled open. Rain flooded through and cooled the yellow ring of heat that glowed on the metal.

One more strike would not only tear a bigger hole in the roof, but also it could break the metal rings that trapped us.

Another tongue of lightning crashed into the container above us, but it managed to squeeze through the narrow gap and forked in two and struck the cuffs that trapped the four of us.

'Why did you save me?' Mother Nature asked as she pried her bindings.

'Because it's not right to leave anyone behind.'

For the briefest of moments, there was a trace of kindness in her eyes. She then jumped up through the hole in the roof, and we followed after her. Mother Nature conjured a green portal and left. The streetlights continued to shine across the street. The truck driver had already left with Verona.

'Hopefully that man from the article can help,' Clara said.

Determination flowed through me. The scent of lemons tickled my tastebuds as the yellow circle of a portal brightened the avenues, even more than the lanterns did. After the three of us stepped inside, Fletcher asked, 'How can he help us?' Worry reflected in his deep blue eyes.

'All I know is that the both of us had and are going

through the same thing.' Lavinia wasn't as confident as I was. Her lack of confidence clouded my mind. If this continued to grow, our emotions would become one. I had to push through her emotions.

The portal spat us outside one of the few older buildings left in Opal Creek. The beige colour of the wood made it glisten in the sunlight. A giant yellow frangipani tree leaned against the ramp; some of its flowers had fallen, and a few had started to turn brown too. On the opposite side were a group of spider lilies. Their long, thin, white petals brushed the edges of the veranda while the other petal that looked like a cupcake liner leaned closer to us. We climbed up the few steps that divided us from the tall glass doors.

Strands of sunlight passed through the doors and onto the photos on the wall. There were pictures from all around the world, from the bustling city of Seoul to the calm, tranquil beaches of the Maldives.

'May I help you?' asked a man dressed in a fuchsia polo shirt with a cream blazer and matching pants. My nerves froze, the answer on the tip of my tongue. *What if he recognises me from the news? Did I get the right person?*

'Are you Herman Kettleby?' Clara asked for me instead.

'Thank you,' I mouthed to her, and she replied with a slight nod of her head.

'Yes, what can I help you with?' Herman inquired.

I looked to Fletcher to help me. 'We were wondering if we could ask you about the time you took your wife to Paris?'

A long pause stretched between us.

'No one has mentioned that for quite some time.'

'Of course. I didn't mean to bring up anything you don't want to revisit.' A floorboard creaked under my foot as I turned away.

A hand reached out from behind me and rested on my arm. 'That doesn't mean that I can't at least try and help you anyway I can.' A smile glowed upon his face. He led us through his brightly lit studio and out to a granny flat out the back that was painted a vibrant apple-green. He slowly stepped down the three steps that separated the deck from the curved line of stone pavers that led to the smaller building. A wind chime with different-sized shells hung above the front door of the granny flat.

Herman reached down into his right pant pocket and fished out a set of keys. They were attached to a retractable cord. It didn't take him long to find the one he needed. Once he unlocked the door, the four of us padded inside. On the right was a kitchenette with a small jar of sugar, and another couple of pots of tea and coffee. On the opposite side was a tiny white fridge covered with magnets from all over the world. For the most part, there were a lot of tropical places that he'd been to: the Cook Islands, Fiji, Vanuatu, Hawaii; there was even one from Mauritius. It was of a dodo bird with an angry look on its face. Below were the words *I used to live here*.

I found it strange that a magnet would say that. Why couldn't it say *Welcome to Mauritius*?

Herman walked over to me. 'Ah, yes, my wife

bought that one.' There was a twinkle of joy in his eyes. 'She thought it'd be funny whenever we have our grandkids over, but they're too clever.' He gestured for me to sit in the area that could only be his living room, where Fletcher had already made himself at home. Herman sunk himself into a mauve armchair with a picture of his wife in a red photo frame and a brown leather photo album. He picked up the frame.

'It was a rainy summer night.'

I sat next to Fletcher on the beige two-seater sofa, while Clara perched herself on the arm next to me. 'I knew that the next day was our wedding anniversary and I still hadn't gotten Connie anything. I felt like everything was being pushed together. When she got home from her job as a receptionist at the dentist's office, she was exhausted and she collapsed onto the sofa. I remembered when we were in high school, she always talked about going to Paris one day, and before I knew it, *POOF!* We were in front of the Eiffel Tower. The sun warmed the back of my neck and Connie was confused about what had happened, and I was too. I could hear the clicks from cameras. People speaking in French. Connie translated for me, since she took French. They asked how we appeared from nowhere? Were we cursed? A few people cried out for the police.'

'So, what did you do?' I asked. The memory of Fletcher and I seeing the news of me being framed for something I didn't commit haunted my brain.

'We booked a night at a little hotel and hid for the rest of the day.' His eyes flicked to Fletcher, who was playing with a small zen garden. 'Look with your eyes, not your hands.' Fletcher dropped the little rake.

'I can't wait my current situation out!' I yelled. 'Did you track down the journalist who wrote that article, N.D. Plume?' This man wasn't much help. Imogen came to the front of my mind again, but I forced myself to not think about her.

'No,' he simply answered.

'Why? It couldn't have been that difficult,' Clara asked. She watched Fletcher as he was about to reach for the rake again, but stopped when he saw her angry stare.

'It wasn't,' Herman responded.

Confusion twisted my face. 'What do you mean?'

'My partner discovered that N.D. Flume was a fake name.'

For the first few seconds, I was disappointed, then I realised that I should've picked up on that simple clue. N.D. Plume was actually 'nom de plume'.

'Don't beat yourself up.' Herman rose from his armchair, picked up his cane and walked over to his kitchenette. He reached to the left and pulled out a few teabags from the box of green tea.

'Sometimes, you just need to rest and gather your thoughts,' he said as he flicked the kettle on and grabbed a couple of mugs from the cupboard that sat above him.

'We haven't really had a proper chance to do that. It's crash in one spot and keep moving after that.'

'Have you explained that it wasn't you who committed that crime at the hospital?'

A sense of urgency spike through my body. I jumped up from the couch as though something burned me.

'How did you know that?'

'I've been able to know when someone with powers is nearby,' he explained as the water in the kettle boiled. It clicked when it was ready to be served.

'Would you like some help?' I asked. Herman tried to find one of the mugs. He touched a mug, and burned his fingers from the heat. I helped without asking further.

'You didn't have to do that, but I appreciate the help.' Herman set down one of the mugs on the small coffee table, and I set the other three down in front of Fletcher and Clara.

'You're welcome,' I said as I turned back and saw that Herman had stepped over to the kitchenette and swept a jar of biscuits from the counter.

The second the biscuit jar was on the table, Fletcher unscrewed the lid and scooped out as many as he could, then he shovelled them in his mouth.

I raised my eyebrows. 'Are you going save some for us?'

He reached over and placed a biscuit where Herman, Clara and I sat, then swiped at least five more treats. A smile curled up my face as laughter started to jump around my chest.

Herman and I made our way around the table back to our seats and rotated the jar so that it faced us. There were a variety of biscuits to choose from: one shaped like a cat, jam and cream, chocolate, a coffee-flavoured one, and a plain one that looked like a phone from before I was born. It was the type of phone where you had to press a number key a certain number of times to get one letter.

Fletcher picked up the phone-shaped biscuit and studied it. 'Were these what phones looked like back in the early two thousands? I saw Mum had stored her old Nokia in the garage. How retro!'

Herman pierced Fletcher with a glare. 'When you hear someone younger than you say to you that the events of your own youth are vintage, let me know.'

He picked up a little black radio that sat in the middle of the table. It reminded me of the one my grandma used to have in her laundry room. She'd often dance to songs that I'd never heard of. This memory made me yearn to reclaim happy times like those. *I will clear my name and return to my family.*

The moment he turned the radio on, Georgina Church's voice squawked through the speakers. She had dreams of becoming a politician. I would never consider her, if I was old enough to vote, not if she were the last person on Earth. In fact, if I had the power, I'd fire her for the simple reason that she didn't have all her facts.

'To international news now, and what appeared to be a peaceful wedding in Tuscany turned into a nightmare. Guests claim to have seen a cosplayer wielding a scythe. Alongside her are an army of people with glowing green eyes.'

Fletcher was still stuffing his face when I directed my attention to him. 'Looks like she got one news report right. Let's go.'

'Okay,' he mumbled around a mouthful of biscuits.

'Thank you for everything, but we have to go.' There has to be a simpler answer than what Herman suggested.

'You're welcome, Ana. If you want to find out more about the journalist who wrote the article on me, there should be a full catalogue at the library. I know it's hard being different. My advice would be to wait it out. Things have a way of coming to an end,' Herman said.

I answered him with a quick nod.

'I'll go to the library. You two deal with her,' Clara suggested as she pointed to the radio.

'Are you sure?' I asked her.

'Don't worry; it won't take me long, unlike Fletcher.' Clara chuckled. She ran back out of the granny flat and toward the photography studio at the front of the house.

Fletcher crossed his arms across his chest.

My eyes closed. A general picture of Tuscany sparked, like I was right there. Something landed in my hands. I opened my eyes and saw a lemon meringue pie. Yellow light erupted through the room. All was silent, until terrified screams cried out through the air.

13: WEDDING TERROR

I was blinded by the brightness of the light that poured cut through the large paned windows.

'Did we miss the reception? I'm starving,' Fletcher moaned.

'You're thinking about food now?' I rolled my eyes. 'You just inhaled all of Herman's biscuits and you're still hungry?'

'I'm a growing man. I need food to be strong.' Fletcher stood there with his arms flexed.

'Will I ever hear the end of this 'man' thing?' I groaned.

Fletcher placed his arm on my shoulder. 'Nope, but that's why you like putting up with me.'

'Sure.'

A stampede of people charged toward us. Fragile items were being destroyed upstairs.

One of the curtains caught fire. Thick, dark grey smoke rose into the sky. Someone poked their head out of the window next to the room that had been sent up in flames. The person's eyes glowed the same eerie green light as Verona's followers in Paris, which meant she couldn't be far away.

The bridal parties had half of their faces painted on as they swarmed down the stairs like a flock of scared birds. They were the easiest to identify with their white satin robes. There was a broken sign that said that the wedding didn't start until sunrise. Jumping to different time zones made keeping up with time extremely confusing, especially since I didn't have a phone.

One of the staff members, a middle-aged, burly man with a thick greyish moustache, complained that people with eyes that glowed green had ruined all of his and his staff's hard work at the marquee at the bottom of the hill.

Speaking of Verona, where is she?

The wedding guests, who were in different stages of dress, charged around us. It was hard to see anything, or anyone. My arm struck the side of one of the large wooden doors. Pain lanced through it, but I didn't have time to fuss over the pain. The pitch-black sky started to fade into the deepest blue. At the bottom of the hill, a yellow glow warmed the top layer of a stone well. I beckoned Fletcher to follow me down to the source of the light.

Two women dressed in white—one in a suit the other in a dress—hurried down the stairwell, their hands entwined with each other.

'What are we going to do? This isn't the wedding I had in mind,' the woman in the suit worried.

The other woman grasped onto her future wife's hands. 'Remember why we decided to marry at sunrise? All I need is you.'

Colour started to fill her panicked face. 'Because all we need is to hope.'

The answer to her wife's question fuelled me with determination to give them a wedding they deserved.

I ran down the hill. It was hard to keep my balance. A few pieces of gravel that lay across the grassy terrain rolled under my shoes. At any time, I could've fallen head over heels down the hill and become tangled in the grape vines.

The well wasn't too far away now. Verona's split ends were highlighted from the glow of the well, while the broken rock fragments gleamed black against the bronze on the shaft of her staff. Verona must've added it after her escape from Paris.

Darkness spread from the tip of her scythe.

'Verona, STOP!'

Her furious eyes cast a wicked glare at me. 'I'm not surprised that you're here, Ana. But I'll never go back to the way I was. I was weak. Why did you think it was easy for me to transform to this? And from the way things are between you and Mother Nature, history will repeat itself.'

'What about the people you have under your spell?'

'They have learned that love is a weakness, but I need more to convince the world. They're foolish enough to cast their dreams and wishes into wells. Do they ever come true?'

I reached out to hold her hand. 'They can if you want them to.'

The rage that swirled in green her eyes turned into hope. There was a chance for me to save her. Verona swallowed the positive emotions.

'You LIAR!' Verona pressed her hands onto her scythe and threw out a finger of lightning from it, which lassoed me and carried me above her. I bit down on my tongue. Pain stung around my arms. I didn't want to give Verona the satisfaction that I was hurting. There was no way she would win. My magic needed to escape, but the static coil didn't allow it to do so. Electricity singed through my denim jacket. I didn't know how much longer I could handle being up here. She let me go. Verona pressed her hands to the sides of her head.

Confusion warped around her face.

Did I get through to the Verona I knew?

I knocked over a row of vines. A bunch of Sangiovese grapes splattered across my jacket.

They were a type of grape used for red wine. Mum showed me a bottle of it once. The back of label read that it was a main ingredient.

'You okay?' Fletcher asked as he ran into me.

'I need to go to a hospital.' A deep gash slashed across my arm. It was a good guess that it was made by the wire that held the vines up.

Verona aimed her scythe at the well. A misty black sphere shot out from it and destroyed the well. A woman screamed from the top of the hill. I saw one of the women in bridalwear as she dropped to her knees. Her partner rubbed her shoulder.

'I'll let you win this time, but next time you won't be so lucky.' Verona's angry expression was the last thing I saw before she and her army vanished in the same dark smoke as before.

'How are you going walk into the hospital? We have no Turkish Delight to help disguise you.'

A picture of a lemon meringue pie was at the front of my mind. It materialised in front of us and almost tipped over. I raised a finger to Fletcher as I used my other hand to pick up the dessert. 'We don't have any yet,' I corrected him. The yellow light from the portal revealed Fletcher's muddled look to my comment.

14: A SIMPLE ANSWER

I teleported us to the first hospital that I could think of. In different circumstances, it wouldn't have been my first choice. Fletcher pulled me toward the sliding glass doors of the hospital's main entrance.

'Come on, I have an idea. Keep your head down; I'm too young to be thrown in jail.' Faith, laughter and a pinch of worry lingered on my face. He saw the concern that I kept hidden deeper than the other emotions. His blue eyes were apologetic in the light of the streetlamps. We slipped inside the building without any suspicions raised.

The hospital was quieter during the night than the day. It might have been because visiting hours were over. Paper snowflakes, made by the children who stayed at the hospital, hung from the ceiling. I couldn't believe the hospital hadn't taken down the Christmas decorations.

Aiden had brought Fletcher and I through a portal weeks after the holiday. It had been longer than a year since I started my new school. I hoped everything would get back to normal so that I could help Mum make my grandma's orange jelly mould. It was the best thing to have in the summer with vanilla ice-cream.

My eyes darted with frantic speed all around the area that we stood in. Once the coast was clear, I stared at a beautiful snowflake made by Hailey, who used a few shades of blue from the lightest being in the centre to a deep navy at the end.

'Over here,' Fletcher yelled, which made me jump out of my dream-like state. He waved at me from in front of a yellow claw machine that was full of a variety of mini chocolates, some I hadn't thought about in a while, especially the ones that were filled with peanuts on the outside and crunchy wafer on the inside.

Fletcher's hands disappeared into his pockets. 'Got any money? This machine is old school and only takes gold coins.'

'We're on the run, Fletcher. Besides, I don't carry any on me. Pretty sure no one does anymore.'

'True.'

'Then why did you ask if you know that not many people carry coins?'

'I don't know?'

I laughed at his answer. A collection of art pieces from the kids hung on the café wall. There was a piece of card with *My Perfect Day* written on it in cursive writing. Was Hailey's on the wall? There were too many to see, so I shuffled back to see them all. As I did, a woman bumped into me wearing a blue-and-white top that reminded me of a sunny day.

'I'm so sorry, I should've watched where I was going,' I apologised. I avoided eye contact with the woman, so that she wouldn't recognise me.

The woman didn't reply with words, she just tapped her ear, then made a cross with her index fingers. She was deaf. Yet another situation I didn't know how to get out of. Wind began to drift through the hospital. I didn't speak sign language.

Fletcher appeared next to me and gestured to woman. He spoke sign language. *I wonder if he can teach me?* The next thing I knew, she was holding out one gold coin. Fletcher tapped a hand to his chin and pointed at the woman.

She signed something back before she walked off.

'That was so cool!' I blurted out.

Fletcher waved a hand at me. 'It was nothing. I took a semester of it the year before you arrived. Now let's get some Turkish Delights, so we don't have to steal from the hospital again, and get someone to look at that arm.' His eyes went straight to my injured arm, which I applied pressure to. He slid the first coin into the machine. His hand flicked the joystick back and forth, eyes full of hunger for the sweet treats. Mine were too.

'How come we didn't ask her?' I asked.

'She wasn't a medical professional. She didn't have a stethoscope round her neck. Also, her ID badge was a visitor's pass.'

'Keen eye,' I answered.

'When your mum works at a hospital, you learn a thing or two.'

Fletcher hit the button to lower the claw down to grab our first group of chocolates, but unfortunately, a lot of them fell from its grasp. These machines had always been rigged. We still had a couple more turns to go. The next attempt went better than the first—we scored a claw full of goods, but no Turkish Delights. Fletcher scooped out our winnings from the machine and divided them between us.

He pushed himself up from the ground. This was it. Our last try. Clouds of nerves gathered in my stomach. Fletcher released a calm breath to help him focus. The claw moved to the back. He dropped the claw into a bunch of Turkish Delights, the most we'd scored so far. The mechanical hand raced over to the sliding drawer that ebbed and flowed like waves at the beach. Fletcher bashed the red button that made the claw drop our last haul onto the tray. The drawer pushed the bunch of sweets to the edge where they would drop into the hole to be collected.

The joy on Fletcher's face could power an entire city.

The pile of candies stopped just before the drop. There were a lot of Turkish Delights right there. Fletcher shook the machine in frustration. Nothing happened. I shared his anger too.

An electric-like current ran through me. A clap of thunder followed as I struck the machine.

The pink-and-gold-wrapped rewards fell down to where Fletcher screamed in happiness.

'That was so cool, just like a rebel from the movies.'

'Thanks,' I replied in a bashful tone.

We unwrapped the delicacies and rubbed them on my face. A couple of nurses wandered on by with strange looks on their faces.

'New beauty treatment, practically makes you look younger,' Fletcher spluttered. The nurses didn't believe him one bit and walked away.

My face started to tingle, just like back in *The Chillin' Penguin*'s bathroom. I scraped the chocolate from my face. It disappeared into tiny white sparkles. 'How do I look?'

'You look like Samantha from *Bewitched*.' Fletcher grabbed a silver serviette box from one of the tables.

'It was what popped into my head in the moment.' I grabbed the reflective box from his hand. My hair was now blond and curled outwards at the bottom. Pale green eyes replaced my brown ones.

'I'm not saying you look ugly.'

'Well, that's a relief.' I gave Fletcher the napkin box and he returned it to the table he got it from. I found Hailey's drawing on the *My Perfect Day* wall. She had drawn herself by the beach with a girl with long black hair. It looked like Imogen. *That's because it is.* I read the description of the art piece: *Me and my best friend Imogen, at the beach.*

Maybe Imogen could help me decide what to do about Herman's advice.

Also, I need someone else to talk to about everything that's happened.

There was only one place I had to be at right that second. The pain from the lightning that charred my waist cried out.

With Fletcher in tow, I walked slowly to the elevator. A chart of all the floors was displayed on the wall next to it. The medical field that specialised in burns was on the same floor that Imogen's room was on. The doors opened and I pressed the button for the third floor. It glowed blue. Before the doors closed, a pale hand stopped in the middle of the path of the doors.

It was the lady from before, the one Fletcher signed with.

She waved at us in greeting. We returned the gesture. Then she signed something I didn't understand.

Fletcher turned his head back at me. 'She asked if you're okay?'

'Tell her I'm fine.' My face scrunched up in pain.

She tilted her head to one side to suggest that she didn't believe me.

'Sarah says that she can take us to a doctor who can look at your injury.'

'Tell her I'm fine, and that I'm also here to see a friend.'

Sarah repeated the same action of disbelief.

I was about to refuse her help when the elevator dinged to let us know that we'd reached the third floor. How did I not hear the other two noises?

We left the elevator and turned the corner. The blue laminated floor was still covered with rainbow-coloured footprints. I was glad to see that not everything had changed. Sarah led us to the reception desk, and I backed away from it like a cat about to touch water.

'It's okay, no one will recognise you, except the three of us,' Fletcher answered. His voice had climbed high with fear like my insides. Before I could find out how she knew I was disguised, a woman with a cheery glow on her face saw Sarah and waved.

'She asked if you know where Uma is?'

The woman with a sunflower pin replied, 'She's on her break if you want to see her.'

The woman made a gesture of her about to bite a sandwich and pointed around the corner. Sarah thanked the woman and we proceeded in the direction the reception lady told us.

I grabbed Sarah's wrist. She stopped and turned back to me. 'What?' she mouthed.

'How did you know that this isn't my real face? Are you loyal to Mother Nature?'

Fletcher translated everything I said to her as I looked out at the darkness beyond the wall of windows. The light from the lampposts shined on some areas, but not all.

'Because I had powers like the two of you do now, and I saw your real face for a second before you turned away,' Fletcher translated.

Fletcher and I were taken aback by what he said.

'What do you mean 'had'?'

Fletcher spoke as the woman continued her story. 'Years ago, I accidentally destroyed my kindergarten when I had a tantrum. My interpreter went to my mum. She is a scientist who studies DNA. They developed a serum to stop the powers completely. Since then, I've been living a normal life putting on puppet shows for deaf children.'

'Ask her if there's any of this serum left.' I hoped

for good news. These powers caused me so many problems. I didn't know how much longer I could hold on. Lavinia screamed at me, which caused me to get a headache.

Sarah shook her head.

A man with black-framed glasses approached us. I was on high alert. Sarah gestured for me to wait and Fletcher told me that he was her interpreter. A sigh of relief escaped me. Sarah knocked on the first door after we turned right down a corridor in the same direction.

An elderly woman poked her head out the door. Grey hair flew out of the bun she'd tied her hair in.

Sarah's interpreter translated what Sarah signed, this time in his deep voice. 'Can you take a look at this girl's injury? I can't stay, I have a show in a little bit.'

'Of course, I don't have anyone until tomorrow.'

Sarah thanked the woman, who I thought might be Uma, and walked away with her interpreter. Before they disappeared around the corner, I yelled, 'What happened to the serum?'

Sarah and her interpreter looked back at me. 'My mum only made enough serum for one person. She thought it was best that I got to lead a normal life.' They headed back in the direction of the elevator.

'Come on in, let's take a look at this injury. Can you wait outside?' Uma asked Fletcher, who nodded.

She asked me to lift my shirt just enough to see the injury on my chest. Grey, studious eyes examined the area. 'How exactly did you get this? Most cases would look much deadlier than these marks.'

'Well, I... umm... got a really big shock from an electric fence on my school's trip to the dairy farm,' I explained on the spot.

Uma jotted my response on a notepad. Her brows were raised in disbelief. I didn't think she bought my story. 'Okay, well, I can give you some cream to soothe the pain, and hopefully the mark will disappear.' She straightened herself and strolled over to a cupboard where she grabbed a box of the same cream my mum used on me anytime I got carpet burn, or even a grazed knee. I lowered my shirt back down again.

She reached for a jar of lollipops. 'Take one, your stomach has been grumbling for five minutes.'

I snatched a strawberry lollipop from the jar, and managed to unwrap it in seconds.

Once I popped my reward into my mouth, my face started to tingle. Uma's facial features churned in fear. 'You're the girl the police are looking for.'

I approached the sink with haste and saw my reflection on the metallic surface. The disguise that Fletcher showed me had faded away. It must've been the strawberry candy.

The elderly doctor picked up the phone. 'Yes, security. I found the girl who committed that crime that Georgina Church talked about on the news. Come quick!'

I raced to the door and ripped it open. 'Fletcher, we got to go. Make her forget we were here and fast!'

A siren screamed all around us. Fletcher went up to the panicked doctor. I turned around as a bright flash of blue shot out of his hand like a camera. We ran away from her office before she could register what had just happened. There were so many corners that we flew by, it was hard to process where we were. Fletcher pulled down on a door handle and shoved me inside without a word. A memory pieced itself together in my brain. Why did this room look familiar?

'Hey guys,' greeted a voice that I hadn't heard in a while.

Imogen's lapis lazuli eyes met my brown ones. The last time we spoke, we had talked about Aiden and shared our grief over his loss. The wall behind her was filled with drawings of Aiden along with handmade cards that occupied the bench by the window.

A knock shook the door. 'Can we come in?' a man with a deep voice asked.

'Just a sec,' Imogen said. 'Hide,' she mouthed to us. Her eyes pointed to Aiden's unused bed.

Without any time to think it over, Fletcher and I tiptoed quickly and tucked ourselves as best as we could under Aiden's bed.

Once Imogen knew that we shouldn't be spotted by anyone else, she allowed the figure behind the door to enter.

'Sorry to bother you, but have you seen the girl who—' the man with the shiny black boots tried to ask, he didn't know how to finish the sentence without hurting Imogen.

Imogen seemed to understand what the man, probably a security officer, was attempting to say. 'No, I haven't seen her.'

'Thank you for your time. Again, I'm sorry to have disturbed you,' the security guard politely replied.

Once the door closed, Imogen gave us the all-clear to come out from under the bed. My whole body ached from being squished under there. Fletcher must've felt it more since he was taller than I was.

'Can someone fill me in on what's going on?'

Fletcher and I looked at each other. How could we explain things when it was hard to even find a place to start from?

'It can't be that difficult to explain,' Imogen continued.

I braved the tense atmosphere that started to brew in the room. 'Well, we've been on the run since Georgina outed me to the world as someone I'm not. I've found out that I have an ancient spirit inside me.' My eyes drifted to the white-squared ceiling. 'I tried to get rid of it, and remade a mirror that's now made Verona evil. I also tried to get answers from people who've been in my shoes before, and now, I don't know what to do?'

I was out of breath after I listed the thoughts that charged around in my head. Imogen poured me a cup of water. It went down my throat in a matter of seconds.

'It seems to me that you need to not take on everyone's advice and think of something no one's thought of before. Just be you.'

'It's not that simple.'

'It is. You're just overwhelming yourself with everyone's stories. You need to write your own.

Here's your chance, look.' Imogen nodded to the T.V. It was another news report.

The reporter was live from the Trevi Fountain. Verona's zombified army protected her as she tapped the blade of her scythe onto the surface of the water.

Blue magical veins spread out across the fountain and spilled out into the cobblestone streets. I watched the tourists run away. The screams filled my ears. I looked at the water and an idea sprouted in my head. *Since the fountain and wishing wells are filled with coins that people bless with wishes, what happens to the water?*

'Don't do what you're thinking. It's too dangerous,' Lavinia warned me.

'I don't need your permission,' I whispered back.

'I've been protecting people like you for centuries. I'm not going to stop now.'

'I can do this myself,' I snapped. The ground began to shake under our feet. Imogen clamped her hands to the sides of her bed. Fletcher's eyes bloomed with concern.

'Are you doing this?' he asked. He flopped over to the bench and held onto the side.

'We don't have much time. Come on.' I lunged over to him and grabbed his hand. 'Thank you,' I told Imogen as the two of us vanished into a cheery yellow portal.

15: AN ARROW IN THE RIGHT DIRECTION

Pain shot through our tailbones as we landed on the bumpy cobblestone path. The fountain was across the road from where the portal spat us out. There wasn't much to see as my view was blocked by the people that ran toward us. There wasn't a cloud in the sky, which on any other day would be a splendid day out, but this wasn't one of those days.

I stood up and braved the storm of panicked citizens and tourists. Every step forward, I was pushed back a few paces. My eyes flicked through the crowd to see if Fletcher had caught up with me. I looked to my right and saw Clara there.

'How did you find us?' I asked.

'It wasn't easy. I had to cast a spell to find your energy, but with the amount of people that have powers in Opal Creek, it was hard to narrow down where you were. My search for this N.D. Plume character came back empty. It's as if they didn't exist until after you and Fletcher came back from travelling through time,' she replied.

'I'm sorry your search was for nothing. Where's Fletcher? I need him.'

'I'm right here,' he said, as he struggled to worm his way through the stampede of people.

Fletcher stood between Clara and I.

'We need to join our powers.' I reached for his hands and started to concentrate on what I needed to do.

Fletcher stared off into nothing. 'What am I supposed to do?'

'We need to create a dome around the fountain that not only helps erase the memories of these people, but to also keep everyone else from listening to our fight.'

I closed my eyes and refocused my breaths. The need to protect the innocent people from Verona flowed from my mind and down to my hands. I hoped that Fletcher had the same thoughts too. He must have, because orange and blue were the only colours I could see from behind my closed eyes.

I opened them to see the marvel that our magic had created. White light glowed bright from under my chin and from Fletcher's dragon ring. The magical artifacts that Verona gave us indicated that our friendship was true. The dark blue veins that she produced from her scythe sizzled to steam as they touched our ankles. Her dark magic had no effect on us.

A giant slice of orange was sprinkled with a bunch of closed blue flowers. They opened and blossomed into forget-me-nots. Tiny flecks of blue rained down on everyone. The crowd around me became calmer, and walked away dazed and confused.

'I'm going to need you to hold the fort while I get Verona back.'

Fletcher opened his now alert eyes. 'How am I supposed to do that?'

'By believing in yourself.'

Lavinia's nerves pulsed through me. 'I don't want to do this. I don't want you in any danger.'

'Thanks, but I've got this.'

Lavinia didn't seem to agree. I felt a sharp pang in my stomach. My hands clutched the area where the pain came from. The ground shook beneath my feet again. Yellow light shined on the path in front of me as a set of brown boots blocked my way.

'Go no further, Lavinia,' Mother Nature said. Her long, dark hair shifted in the light breeze.

'I'm—I don't have time for this. I need to save a friend.'

'Nice excuse. You remember Clarence, I trust?'

A boy with chestnut brown hair stood out from behind Mother Nature. His palms glowed pink.

'Watch out! Clarence is part of the Council of One, a group of people with more than one disability. Their power is to take away from others,' Lavinia warned me.

Clarence threw a bolt of energy at me. I dodged it.

He tried again. I wasn't ready, but I rolled out of the way just in time for his magic to hit a tree behind me, which turned into a man.

'How long have I been like this?' the former tree man asked.

Anger erupted behind Mother Nature's eyes as she glared at the tree man. 'You haven't completed your punishment yet!'

The pink light had come at me for a third time. It was about to hit my face when Clara shoved me out of the way. The light struck her and disappeared before something purple flowed out of her like a waterfall.

'Go, I'll be okay.'

Tears were spilling down my cheeks.

'NO! How could you?' Mother Nature roared.

'You're losing control of yourself, Elizabeth. She hasn't.'

The orange dome that I formed started to glitch. I couldn't break down now. I had to keep going.

For Verona.

For the world.

For me.

Every step I took was harder than the last. Lavinia wanted me to pull back, but I couldn't. I'd come this far, and I was determined to save my friend.

Indigo light continued swim out of the fountain from Verona's scythe. The cords of light passed through the barrier and formed into charcoal-grey ghost-like people, except with really long fingernails, which they calmly stroked against innocent bystanders' temples. Then the strange new creatures whispered something into people's ears.

Two of Verona's zombified followers snuck up behind me and grabbed my arms. Both of them were slim, but strong. I was forced to go where they went. The rest of Verona's followers moved aside as we went toward the fountain. Once there, Verona told them to keep everyone else occupied while the two of us had a chat.

The surface of the water in the iconic landmark looked like a sunny day with its rich blue and clear tones. It reflected the bright colours from Fletcher's and my shield.

'Beautiful, isn't it? But it's time to make everyone who made a wish in a well experience the other side of their hopes and dreams.' Verona stared longingly at the water.

'I won't let you do that. The world needs love,' I said determined, even though the ground still shook.

'I know you think that, but it's time for the world to seek their darkest desires.' Verona reached into a silver pouch tied at her hip and didn't pull out coins, but something I thought was lost.

The Mirror of Harmony.

I stared at its crystalline reflection. 'How did you find that?'

'When everyone was gone, I went back and got it in case you tried to stop me from destroying my former home. That's what'll happen when I show the other side to people's wishes. No wishes of love will mean bye-bye to the fairy realm.'

Something burned in my chest like thousands of wasp stings. I pressed my hand to the sore area. A bright, ghostly figure started to pull away from me. It had no distinct features, yet there was something about it that was familiar. I kept my eyes on the mirror's ethereal surface. The pale being refused to leave my side.

'Ana, please! Together, we can free Verona. I don't want to leave you,' Lavinia cried out.

Her voice came from the same direction as the familiar ghost. Lavinia's voice didn't echo in my head anymore.

My face strained as it searched for an answer. 'What's happening?'

'Why, that's the Mirror of Harmony working its magic. I can't very well have the two of you stopping my plans.' Verona gestured to me and the white energy figure that stood next to me. *The thing next to me is Lavinia?* The sensation that burned in my chest started to wither away.

'Please, I don't want to leave you. I need you,' Lavinia pleaded next me. Her luminous outline moved her arms away from her side and back to the side of her body again.

Beside me were a few coins that formed a bow and arrow. 'Who said I'd need Lavinia for my plan to succeed?' The clear quartz lens of the mirror glowed brighter, as did the confident smile that gleamed across my face.

Verona's anger darkened her face. This wasn't the way she imagined her plan would go.

I plunged my hands into the constellation of coins and pushed myself from the cold pool. White light glowed from my chest and rippled through the cloudy basin.

With the help of my newfound confidence, a ripple of white magic pushed Verona and Lavinia away from me. *No one can tell me what to do.* The spiritual form solidified into a human with wild orange-red curls that fell freely down her back. A dress of blue cotton hugged her body while straps of tiny multi-coloured flowers held up the garment.

She looked into my eyes and screamed, 'What did you do that for?'

I stared at her pale green face. 'Because you don't control me. I make my own destiny.'

The mirror that Verona held burned her hand and it shattered into pennies and shards of crystal.

My hands glowed orange as I crunched the silver coins in my hand. A stream of liquid metal curved either side of my closed fist. When they stopped, a bow was formed.

'Lavinia?' Mother Nature held her arms against a couple of Verona's army. She then wrapped them in vines.

The green-skinned girl turned to see Mother Nature's furious gaze.

'The magic of the wishing well coins and the quartz have separated you from Ana. Which means you have no one to keep you safe. You will never be Mother Nature—that role is mine.'

The earth cried out in pain and a crack appeared in between them.

An awkward gap of tension filled this moment. Now was my chance to make my move.

The water wasn't filled with the dark blue magic anymore. Verona was on the ground a few metres away.

'You purified the water. How?' Verona asked, enraged.

'All I had to do was reclaim who I was before I

found out about Lavinia.'

An elderly woman in a green dress approached from behind me. 'And it's because you have a pure heart and spirit.'

This was the same woman whom I spoke to back in Victorian London. The one who told me about the lonely tree on the island in the middle of the lake.

'Mother? What are you doing here?' Lavinia and Mother Nature asked in unison.

'I'm here to save my family from destroying the world.' She looked at me. 'You take care of Verona while I have a chat with my daughters.' Her voice was kind, but also had a bite of determination to it.

The woman in emerald walked away. I was left with a bow and no arrow. My eyes scanned the bottom again. Tiny fragments of metal shined all the way on the opposite side of where I stood. They sparkled like miniature stars underneath the statue that held a trident.

Verona flopped over to face me. 'Stop her!'

With one jump, I splashed into the basin. The cold water soaked not just my jacket sleeve, but my jeans too. At least they'd be washed. I waded through the water as fast as I could. Verona barked at a man and woman from her army to chase after me. They were faster than I was.

The man reached out to grab me, but I swerved to the right and scooped up the coins.

The sandstone statues were mere inches from my face. There was nowhere to go but up. I shoved the coins in my pocket and shuffled up onto one of the horses on the end.

Just like when I made the bow, the coins melted in my hands. Once the slim, metallic arrow was forged, I had one last problem. My arrow needed feathers at the end.

An idea whispered to me. I listened to it. When Verona became evil, dark magic chopped off her hair. *Maybe I could use magic to try and locate her hair?* I closed my eyes and pictured the Emerald Mountains, the last place where Verona had long hair. An image of her loose hair caught under some rocks below the cliff drew itself in front of my eyelids.

Desperation fried my brain as that bunch of hair appeared in my hand. A silver light glowed around my hand when I squeezed it. I uncurled my hand and saw brown feathers in place of the hair. Once my fingers placed them around the arrow, they stuck to the end.

Remember what you were taught at grade five camp in archery. Take your time.

I nocked the arrow in the bowstring that revealed itself, as if the bow could sense the arrow. Even though the bowstring was a cord of honey-coloured lightning, it didn't sting me.

Breathe. My fingers gripped the arrow on both sides. I slowly took some deep breaths in and out. No one could distract me from my task.

Aim. Once I focused on the task I had to complete and nothing else, I raised the bow and arrow at Verona.

Fire. I released the arrow. The couple that was sent

to chase me tried to jump in front of the arrow's path. I knocked them down with a couple of light breezes. The arrow passed through Verona's heart, just as she stood up. The fairy clutched her heart as the arrow landed behind her.

A powerful burst of energy pulsed from Verona. Her dress changed back to red and her hair grew back to its long, flowy self again. The scythe was melted down in a puddle of bronze metal. Verona's followers pressed their hands to their heads, with no idea where they were, or how they came to be in Rome.

The earth still cried out in pain as Mother Nature and Lavinia continued to fight. I shuffled back across the Trevi to where the woman seemed to be having no luck with her daughters' argument.

The memory from when I first touch the Earthshifter floated back to me.

'That's it.' I walked over to Lavinia and Mother Nature as they fought again.

'What's it?' their mother asked as she quickly scurried over to where we were.

'Grab Mother Nature's hand,' I instructed her as I reached for Lavinia's. A bright yellow light followed after us.

We landed in the Archives at school. Luckily, no one was there.

'Where have you taken us?' Mother Nature asked. Confusion coloured her eyes.

'There's something you both need to see.' The opalescent light from the wall shimmered still from when I touched it the last time and saw the memory of how the mirror was separated. *Guess the mirror's magic took some time to fully clear away from my mind.*

'Is that our Tunneller? The one we used to sneak out and see this world?'

'Before, you took my powers and gave them to disabled people, instead of your own.'

Fury boiled behind Lavinia's eyes. 'I was trying to help them defend themselves.'

'Without asking? You put our world in danger,' Mother Nature hissed.

'Can you girls go back to being friends?' their mother asked. 'What you did wasn't right, Lavinia. I understand that you wanted to help others, but it put a lot of others in grave danger.'

The victorious smile creased Mother Nature's face. Their mum saw it.

'Don't be quick to celebrate, Rootha. You not only used dark magic, but you also framed this poor girl for something she didn't do. Now release this woman whose body you currently are inside of, and let her see her daughter,' she advised.

'Yes, mum.' Mother Nature touched a part of the light-filled wall. She separated herself from Elizabeth. The craft must be made of the same crystal as the mirror.

Elizabeth's eyes met mine and they reminded me of Charlotte. 'I forgive you,' was all she said before she rose to the ceiling and disappeared. A tear crept forward to my eye. I let it fall.

'Mum, I just wanted for disabled people to be able to protect themselves. Isn't that admirable?'

'It is, but remember that your father chose Rootha because she was the right choice to help us Florians thrive.'

'I wasn't going to let disabled people suffer. But we can't put ourselves in line of the lives of humans,' Rootha explained.

Lavinia was lost for words. 'I'm sorry. I didn't know.' The earthquake started to settle. 'Give me your hand, Ana.' She extended her hand to me. 'What would you like to suggest we do?'

'I would let people decide if they want powers or not, and I'd like to go home.'

'So be it.' Lavinia linked hands with her sister, their mother and me. A forget-me-not-blue light blossomed in front me. The ground stopped its tantrum and went quiet, then an image of the willow tree from the park Fletcher and I went to stood in front of me. I wasn't the one who thought of the tree. The three women thanked me and happiness radiated around them.

The blue light washed over us before the three green-skinned women closed their eyes and turned into balls of energy and dissolved through the portal. My magic flowed out of me with them. I chose to let it go. Clouds gathered above the willow tree and rain drizzled down to its roots. The faint blue light covered the tree for a second. The pastel-coloured magic escaped out of the tree and passed through the park, but it danced around me.

The image of the tree vanished.

I didn't have the energy to stand. Darkness covered my eyes as I fell to ground, asleep.

An alarm clock, with a purple dragon that slept atop it, begged me to get up. I slammed the button down and crawled under the warm covers of my bed.

My bed.

My eyes sprung open, and I launched out of bed. My legs were a little shaky. Next time, I wouldn't do that. My feet propelled me forward to the dining room where Mum had just made breakfast, and Dad sat with his morning newspaper and coffee.

I jumped behind Dad and squeezed him. His coffee sloshed onto his white shirt. He wasn't mad about it.

'Good morning to you, spring bean. What's got you so happy?' he chuckled.

'Can't I just be happy to see my parents?' I unclasped my arms from Dad and hugged Mum.

It was nice to see their faces happy and not sad like when I last saw them.

'Did you hear Georgina Church was fired from her job for making up some silly story about you at the hospital committing a crime? She needs to get her facts straight.'

A warm feeling swelled through me.

'Err, yeah, she really does.'

'Why are you still in your PJs, sweetheart? Dad's going to drop you off for your first day of your second year of high school.'

I looked down at my zodiac sleepwear. 'Oh, sorry. My mind must be on a different planet or something.'

After I changed into my uniform and had an amazing fruit salad with yoghurt and chia seeds that Mum prepared, I hopped into dad's light blue station wagon. I'd never been this excited about going to school. Nerves tickled across my arms, but there was no wind to follow them. Relief flowed from my heart.

As Dad parked the car in front of the short chain-link fence that separated the school from the real world, I took a big, anxious breath in.

'Excited about year eight?' Dad asked. My worries fizzled away.

'Among other things, yeah,' I answered. He reached back and dragged my beige backpack between the front seats.

'What book did you pack today?' Dad's face strained under the weight of my bag.

'It's about a young girl who gets chosen to fulfill an ancient prophecy.'

'Does it have a happy ending?'

'I think it will.'

'If you say so. I'll pick you up at three, okay?'

'Okay, Dad.'

I climbed out of the car, closed the door and waved as the car drove off.

My hand reached for the lock on the gate just as someone else did.

The person's bright red hair gave away who it was.

'Hey, what happened to you after you disappeared with those three ladies?' Fletcher asked.

'I just wanted for people like me to choose if they want their powers. Then I blacked out.'

'It must have released a memory wipe worldwide because no one wants to hunt you down.'

'What's weirder is that I think I don't have my

powers anymore.'

'Huh, well—'

The sound of the school bell cut Fletcher off mid-sentence and alerted everyone that the day had just begun.

'Want to be late again?' he asked as a cheeky grin crawled up his face.

I chuckled. 'You know what happened last time, right?'

My hand flipped the latch on the gate up and I used my hip to push it open. A gust of wind picked up out of nowhere and pushed us into the school. *Where did that wind come from?* It couldn't have been me because I gave up my powers. Fletcher and I crashed into a group of senior students.

'Sorry,' I apologised to them.

The gate slammed shut behind us.

'Come on, class is about to begin.' I tagged Fletcher on his shoulder as he chased after me to our first class.

Acknowledgements

I can't believe after so long I finally have written a trilogy of books. The drafting process of writing Twisted Roots was hard, since I lost my mum last year. So with that said, Mum I want to thank you for all the things you taught me about life and always seeing me for who I truly am. I love you and miss you so much. I hope you're proud of me.

To the rest of my family and friends, thank you for supporting me in my journey to becoming not only an author, but a better person each day. To L.L. Hunter, thank you for helping me come up with the title for the final book. To Annie McCann, you have been like a sister to me, always including me in everything, and without you I would never have been on an author panel. To H.M. Hodgson and Jacqueline Hayley thanks for taking me under your wing at my first solo book event. To all the other authors I have met at book conventions, there's too many to name, thank you for your advice and support. A massive thank you to all the bookstores that stock my books, it means the world to see my books in stores. To Shayla Morgansen, thank you for our catch ups and your kind words.

To Ouroborus Book Services, thank you for seeing something in my work so that I can share my message to the world. To Sabrina RG Raven, thank you for the amazing covers over the years. To Kirsty Inic and Rachel Marchesi, thank you for all of your help editing my books. I will carry your advice into my future books. To my support worker, Nikki, thank you for keeping me grounded when I need it and for lifting me up any time I need it. I also want to thank Sue Lynn Tan, who's books helped me through my mum's passing.

Finally, to the readers, thank you for picking up my books and giving them a chance. I know that with your help we can make the world a more inclusive space.

ABOUT THE AUTHOR

J.J. Fryer was born in South Brisbane and moved to the Sunshine Coast when he was six months old. He was born with Mild Cerebral Palsy and later diagnosed with Asperger's Syndrome in June, 2008. J.J. loved fantasy from a young age. He discovered his flair for writing at 17 and hopes to go far with his writing. He has been an extra on Mako: Island of Secrets and Harrow. His debut series, Beneath the Surface hopes that it will inspire people with Special needs to believe in themselves. In his spare time he loves to read, geek out to his favourite movies and T.V. shows and goes on the occasional walk in nature.

Follow J.J. Fryer

Facebook: J.J. Fryerauthor
Instagram: @jjfryerwritesrandom
Twitter: @jjfryer_09
www.ouroborusbooks.com

www.ingramcontent.com/pod-product-compliance
Lightning Source LLC
LaVergne TN
LVHW031606060526
838201LV00063B/4748